D1615778

The Jealous Lover

Also by Larbi Layachi

A *Life Full of Holes* (1964)
Yesterday and Today (1985)

The Jealous Lover

by Larbi Layachi

TOMBOUCTOU BOOKS

Cover from a painting by Duane Big Eagle.
Portrait of the author by Neil Sampson.
Typography by Rock & Jones.

Chapter two appeared in Howard Junker's
ZYZZYVA magazine, Vol. I, No. 2.

Library of Congress Catalog Card Number: 85-52108

ISBN 0 939180-30-8

Note

I first met Larbi Layachi at the San Francisco Community College in 1979 in a program coordinated by Kathy Kerr-Schochet. Larbi was a student in my English grammar and writing classes. It didn't take long for me to see that Larbi was a writer. He had a gift for stories. We began to work together on a book Larbi wanted to write. We would sit in his small apartment, drink jasmine tea with lots of sugar, and Larbi would speak his book out to me in English. He carried all the words in his head and seldom lost his place. I wrote down exactly what he said and read it back to him. Later we would sit in his backyard among yellow tea roses, green beans and sweet basil and enjoy the light.

—Katharine Harer

I am dedicating this book to thirteen fine people for being so helpful to me. It's nice to know there are still good people in the world.

Helen Susan Gross
Michael J. Gross
Deborah Susan
Mrs. Grace Covello
Kathy Kerr-Schochet
Nancy McKee-Jolda
Kimi Sugioka
Katharine Harer
Valerie Saunders
Marlene Raderman
Nuha Shatara
Ira Yeager
William F. Owen

Chapter One

I Wasn't Cold

N o," he said. "I can't let him study here any more and I can't give him any more of my food. He can go out and work."

"Even if he goes out and looks," said my mother, "he's not going to know where to go to get work."

He said: "It's not my business what he does, but he can't stay here without working."

I went to work on the beach, helping the fishermen pull in their nets.

And at home my mother and the man were always fighting about me.

I would go in the morning and pull on the nets until the end of the afternoon. They gave me two rials. If they caught a lot of fish, they gave me three, but that was not very often.

I was about ten years old, and I lived with my mother and her husband in a little house on the dunes near the tobacco factory. One day I had been pulling in the fishermen's nets for them all day long. In the afternoon when my work was finished I came home and found my young brother back from school.

"Ah, Mohammed? Has vacation begun? Or not yet?"

"No. Tomorrow's the last day of school."

"Now you'll be able to go to the beach with me and swim every day."

"Yes," he said. "That will be good."

"Come on," I told him. "We'll go to the beach now and see if we meet somebody who has a ball."

We went to the beach, and there were no other boys there at all. It was almost sunset. Just a few fishermen sitting on the sand and leaning against the boats, talking.

"Let's go home," I said.

We went back home. We found my mother getting dinner, and we sat down to wait. When she had finished making the food, she brought it in and put it on the taifor. And she cut the bread and brought the bowls. "Now come and eat," she said.

We ate our dinner and went to sleep.

In the morning I got up early, put a piece of bread into my pocket, and went to the place on the beach where they pulled in the nets. Everyone else in the house was still asleep.

I worked all day, and we caught many fish. The days when that happened, the chief of the fishermen always gave whatever was in the last netful to the men and boys who were working with him, and each one went home with a lot of fish. That day he paid me five rials and gave me a basketful of fish.

Ths has been a good day, I thought. I carried the basket of fish, walking across the sand dunes until I got to our orchard.

My mother was there. When I put the basket down, she said, "Aoulidi, what have you got in the basket? Have you brought some fish?"

"Yes. They're there in the basket. The chief gave us tajine for lunch today."

She took the fish out and put them onto a tray. And then she began to get them ready for dinner. I was going to go out and play.

"Where are you going?" she asked me.

"Just outside."

"Did you bring any money today?"

"Yes. I brought some."

"How much?"

"Five rials."

"Give them to me," she told me. "And I'll put them here until my husband comes home."

I took out the five rials and gave them to her. And I went outside. I walked around in the orchard and pulled up weeds and threw them away. After I had been there a little while, my brother came.

"Well!" I said. "Has the vacation begun?"

"School's finished," he said. "We're free now."

He went into the house and I stayed outside working. A few minutes later my mother's husband came home. I went and kissed his hand as he was going through the door into the house, and then I went in after him.

My mother was busy getting dinner, and my brother and I were talking together. Sometimes my mother's husband would say a word or two to us. He did not like his son to talk with me or play with me, because he was sending him to school. He wanted him to grow up to be an important man. He would say to my mother: "Keep your son away from my boy. He's going to ruin him."

When she had finished making dinner, my mother said:

"Come on and eat."

We ate our dinner. Afterward Mohammed said to his father: "Tomorrow I'm going with Larbi to the beach. He'll pull on the nets and I'll swim near him."

"No. You're not going with him. You're not old enough to go there. You'll stay home and he'll go and do his work."

"Ouakha."

The next day I got up, washed my face, and put a piece of bread in the pocket of my jacket. Then I walked up the beach until I got to the place where they pulled in the nets, and sat there waiting for the rest of the men to come and put the nets and ropes and corks into the boat. When eveything was in it, we pulled it out into the water. The fishermen jumped into the boat and threw the end of the rope overboard. A man took it and went to the shore. Then the others rowed out into the bay. We went back to the beach and sat down. A little later I saw Mohammed running down to the edge of the water, to where I was sitting.

"Mohammed! Why did you come?"

"I came to swim," he said.

"And in the afternoon your father's going to yell at me. He's going to think I told you to come."

"No," he said. "I'm not going to stay until afternoon. I'm going home at noon."

"Yes. If you go back at noon, see if Mother has any food ready, and bring me back some."

The fishermen threw out the net and came back to the shore with the rowboat. We took hold of the rope at the end of the net and began to pull on it. And Mohammed was swimming and playing in the sand. After a while he began to walk around, and then he came over and started to pull on the net too. The chief came and patted him on the head. He was laughing.

"Who's this boy?" he said.

"My brother," I told him.

"Yes? He works? Or what does he do?"

"No, he doesn't work. He learns. He goes to school."

The chief walked away. Mohammed stayed beside me, pulling on the rope. And we went on tugging at it. When I would get up onto the sand where a fisherman was rolling the rope into a ball, I would unfasten my belt from the rope and run back down into the water. Then I would hitch my belt onto the rope again and start pulling. And when I changed places, Mohammed changed with me and began pulling again. There were many people, forty or fifty of them in a line, all pulling on the net. It came in very slowly. And we went on like that until lunch time.

Mohammed said: "Brother, I'm going home and eat. I'm hungry."

"Yes. Go on," I told him. "If there's enough food for me, bring me back a little of it inside a piece of bread."

"Ouakha." He went home.

He went to the house and ate his lunch. Then he put some boiled potatoes inside a piece of bread and brought them back to me.

"Is that all you ate at the house?" I asked him.

He said: "No. We ate a little fish too."

"Allah hiaouddi! Couldn't she have sent me even one fish?"

"Take it."

I took the food from him and ate it. When I had finished eating, the rowboat came in from the bay, dragging the rope of the net behind it. We began to work again, and Mohammed pulled too. Pulling, pulling, until we had brought in two more nets. Then the chief said: "That's it. That's enough for today."

We gathered up the nets and ropes and oars, and we pulled the boat up onto the sand. Then we went to the shack where we got paid. The chief gave each one his money. When he paid me, Mohammed was standing beside me. The chief took out a rial and gave it to him.

"Take this," he said. "You worked today at the nets with the rest of us."

Mohammed took the rial. "Look! He gave me a rial."

"Good."

"This rial, you take it," Mohammed said. "You don't eat lunch at home. Maybe you'll want to buy something."

"Ouakha," I said. I took the rial from him and put it away in my pocket. When I went home my mother's husband was there.

"Well. Perhaps you've brought some money with you," he said.

"Yes. He paid me three rials."

"On a fine day like this? No wind or anything? Only three rials?"

"That's what he gave me," I said. "Only three rials."

A little later Mohammed came in.

"Where have you been all day?" his father asked him.

"Nowhere. Just here, playing."

"Be sure you don't go with Larbi to the place where they pull in the nets. Remember what I told you."

"I won't go with him," said Mohammed.

My mother's husband put the three rials into his pocket and sat down. My mother came in.

"You've got to go and buy something for dinner," she told him.

He went out to the bacal and came back with some food. My mother began to prepare the meal. Mohammed and I went into the other room and played checkers. Then my mother came and said:

"Come and eat now."

And we sat down and ate. We drank tea afterward and talked a little, and then we went to bed. Mohammed slept inside with my mother and her husband, and I slept outside in the shed. It was warm, and so the donkey was out in the orchard. When it was cold he slept in the shed with me.

I went to sleep that night. And in the morning I got up and washed my face, took a piece of bread, and went out to the beach to work. The men who pulled the nets were coming along the shore. When the chief got there, we pulled the boat across the sand and down into the waves. We put everything into it, and the fishermen rowed out into the bay. We pulled the first net in. While we were pulling in the second, Mohammed came along.

"Ah, Mohammed! So you came!"

"Yes," he said.

"Was your father at home when you went out?"

"No. He's gone to the city."

"Good."

Then he said: "I'm going to stay and work with you all day."

"No," I told him. "You're too little."

"Even if I am, I can pull. And maybe the chief will give me something again, like yesterday,"

He took hold of the rope and began to tug on it as we were doing. He was small. All he could do was pull a little, and it did not help at all. He stayed all day with me and did not go home to lunch. And when the afternoon was over, the chief said: "Now spread the nets to dry and pull up the boat."

The chief went ahead to the shack, and we followed him.

He paid us, and I got five rials. Then he took out two more rials. "Take these," he told Mohammed. "You stayed all day working."

"Ah, brother! Two rials today!"

"I'm hungry," I said. "We'll buy some bread and some tuna fish, and eat here. Then we'll go home."

"Ouakha."

I went into a bacal and bought a loaf of bread and a can of tuna fish. I opened the bread and put the fish inside. We went over to a row of cactuses and sat down in the shade behind them. We started to eat, and we went on eating until we had had enough, and then we got up.

"How much did you pay for the food?" said Mohammed.

"A rial," I told him.

"Here," he said. "Here's the rial you spent for the food. We'll keep the other rial. Maybe some day we'll be working at the beach and we'll need money for food. Take it and save it."

We walked to our orchard. Then I went inside. My mother was there. I kissed her hand.

"Ah, aoulidi! Did you bring any fish today or not?"
"No."
"And your brother Mohammed? Haven't you seen him?"
"He's playing with the Spaniards."
"He hasn't been home all day."
"He hasn't?"
"That's right."
"I don't know where he's been," I told her.
"Are you sure he wasn't with you?" she said. "If his father comes home and asks him, and he says he was with you, he'll beat you both."
I said: "No. He wasn't with me."
A little later Mohammed came in. "Mother! Mother! Give me something to eat. I'm hungry."
"Why haven't you come back before this?" she said. "You've been gone all day, and now you come and say you're hungry."
"I was playing with the boys."
And I was looking at him, and I was afraid he was going to say he had been with me.
"You'll have to be careful," she said. "Your father asked where you were, and I told him you hadn't come home to eat. When he comes, you'll have to take care of yourself."
We walked a while then. And soon my mother's husband came in. He said: "So, boy! Where were you this noon?"
"I was playing with the Nazarenes," said Mohammed.
"Yes? You were playing with the Nazarenes?" He grabbed him and gave him three slaps in the face. "I swear to Allah, if you don't tell me truth, tonight I'll tie you up and beat you to death."
"I was with Larbi pulling on the nets."
"You were with Larbi pulling on the nets?"
"Yes."
"You're so big you can pull on the nets?" Then he said to me:

"When you saw him there, why didn't you tell him to come home?"

I said: "He came, and I told him to go home. I said you'd yell at him if he stayed, but he said you were his father and it would be all right. So he stayed."

Then he grabbed me and hit me. "Go outside!" he shouted.

I went out and began to walk around in the orchard in the dark. After an hour had gone by, still nobody had called me.

"Ah!" I thought. "Now I have no place to sleep tonight. But it's not cold. I'll go over under that tree and lie down."

I went over and lay down in the dirt under the tree. It got very late. I could see the lights in the house, so I knew they were not asleep there. Then my mother came out and began to call: "Larbi! Larbi!"

I pretended I was not there. She went on calling, and after a while I said: "What?"

"Come here!"

I got up and walked into the shed to my mat. I lay down. My mother went and got a little food and brought it to me. I ate it and then I went to sleep.

In the morning I got up, washed my face, put a piece of bread into my pocket, and went out. I walked to the place where the nets were, and when we had pushed the rowboat down to the water and it was ready to go out, my head began to hurt.

And the boat went out with the net in it, and they threw the net into the water. The men were pulling on the rope. And my head was hurting me very much. I got up and took hold of the rope with them. But I could not pull. I only had my hands on the rope and was walking along with them.

One of the fishermen said: "Pull, Larbi! Pull! What's the matter with you? Are you weak today? Your hand is just lying on the rope. You're not pulling at all."

I told him: "By Allah the blessed, my head hurts me!"

"If your head hurts, go to the chief and tell him. Don't work today."

"No. Just leave me alone."

And I stayed working all day, but I felt sick. And at the end of the day I had to walk very slowly.

I got to the shack where the chief was, and he paid me three rials, and I started home. When I went in, my mother looked at me.

"What's the matter, boy?"

"Nothing. My head aches, that's all."

"And were you able to work or not today?"

"Yes, I worked. Here are three rials."

I gave her the money and went to my mat in the shed and lay down. Soon my mother's husband came in. Mohammed was with him. They had been in the city together.

My mother's husband looked at me. He called to my mother: "What's the matter with this one? Why is he lying down?"

"His head hurts him," he said.

He had brought food with him, and he gave it to my mother. When she had finished cooking it, she brought a little to me. They ate in the other room. I finished my dinner and fell asleep while they were talking.

And I slept, and in the morning I could not lift my head off the mat. My mother's husband got up, and found me still lying there.

"Ha, Larbi! Aren't you going to pull on the nets today?"

"By Allah, I don't feel well. I can't go today."

"Just get up, that's all, and go outside. When you feel the air, you'll be able to go."

I tried to get up, but I could not stand on my legs. My knees were empty.

I said: "I can't even move."

And I stayed there. And my mother got up and made me some harira. She brought me a bowl of it, and I ate it.

A little later her husband went into town to the market. At noon my mother made lunch. She brought me some.

"Take it. Eat," she told me.

"No. I don't want anything."

"Just eat a little."

"I can't."

And I stayed that way. I ate no lunch, and when dinner time came I ate no dinner. And it began to rain. That night it rained a great deal. It was raining at twilight, and it kept raining more and more. I was listening to it fall on the tin roof over my head. In the night, they slept, and the rain kept falling.

When it was morning my mother got up and made breakfast. Her husband came out to the shed and said: "Come on! Get up! Aren't you going out? The fresh air will give you strength. All you do is lie in bed. How are you going to get better?"

"What am I going to do?" I said. "I can't even move, and you want me to get up and go out? And it's raining. Where am I going in the rain?"

I drank a little coffee, and stayed lying on the mat in the shed all day. And the rain kept falling.

And at twilight my mother said: "Si Abdallah, bring the donkey in. Here it's been raining all this time on him. He stayed in the rain all last night and all day today. Bring him inside."

Her husband went outside and got the donkey and let him into the shed. He tied him in a corner across from the mat where I was lying.

My mother made dinner and brought me some.

"Don't you want to eat a little?"

"No, I can't."

And they sat down to eat, my mother, her husband and Mohammed. She made tea and they drank it. And they slept, and the rain was falling everywhere around us. It went on raining all night.

In the morning there was a little light. I saw that the water was beginning to come in under the door of the shed.

My mother got up. She came to the door and looked.

"Si Abdallah! Get up! Get up! The water's going to come in on top of us."

"No, yaouddi! The water won't come in."

"Get up! It's coming in. Get up and dig a trench outside the door."

"It won't come in," he told her.

After a while he got up. He took a hoe and began to make a trench in the earth outside the door of the shed.

The rain kept coming down. We stayed in the house, and it went on raining. My mother got breakfast. After they had eaten, she came and asked me: "Shall I make you a little harira?"

"Yes. I think I can eat a little harira."

She made some soup and brought it to me in a bowl. And I took three or four sips, and gave the bowl back.

"Here, Mother. That's enough for me. I can't even move."

I could not move, and I was very cold. The blanket over me was made of four sugar sacks, but it was not enough, and it was wet. Every minute or so there were drops of water coming through the roof. They fell on the donkey and on me.

I thought: Ehi aloudi! The rain everywhere, and the cold, and on top of that I'm sick, and I can't even move.

It did not stop raining. In the afternoon my mother's husband came and said: "I'm going to the market."

He went to the market and bought a few fish. He brought them back to my mother, and she made dinner. But I did not want anything.

"If it rains all night again," said my mother, "the water's going to come into the house."

"And if it does, what are we supposed to do?" said her husband. "Where are we supposed to go?"

She did not answer.

Then he said: "I can build a platform out of planks, and we can put the bed on top of it. We won't sleep on the floor tonight. If the water come in, we'll be dry."

He took some planks and some nails and some rope, and began to build a platform. And he went on working until he had finished it. He made it as high as a table. Then he came out into the shed to make me a platform. He put planks on top of two big square tin cans, and I slept on the planks. One can was under my feet. My mother came and said: "Now go to sleep."

And I slept there, and they slept inside. Half the night I slept. Then in my sleep I turned over and my arm fell into the cold water.

I put my hand down into the water. It was deep.

I began to call: "Ah, Mother! Ah, Mother!"

"What is it?" she said.

"The water's come in over us."

She got up and lighted a lamp with a match, and she saw the shed full of water.

"Get up! Get up! she told her husband. "Here's the water inside with us." He sat up. "And where do you expect to go?" he asked her. "It's the middle of the night and the water's all around us, and you want to go out? We'll just stay here and see if it comes up as high as the bed."

"It's almost up to my bed now," I said.

"Where am I supposed to put you?" he said. "If the water's almost up to you, where am I going to put you?"

I sat up and stayed where I was, sitting on the planks. The lamp was still burning, and the rain was making a lot of noise, and the water was coming in fast. It was getting higher, and it began to touch the boards where I was sitting.

I called out: "Azizi!"

"What is it?" he said.

"The water's up to the planks."

"What can I do about it? If you can get outside, go on out. You can find a doorway somewhere, maybe."

This is bad, I thought. Where can I go? It's raining. I'd better stay here. I can squat so that only my feet will be wet. If I go out, I'll be wet all over.

And I stayed crouching like that on top of the boards until it began to get light outside. When it was morning my mother got up and came through the shed. The water there was up to her knees. She opened the door into the orchard. It was still raining. The water was deep in the orchard, and there was water everywhere.

She went back into the room.

"Si Abdallah," she said to her husband. "The world is full of water. You can't see anything but water."

He got up and put on his djellaba. Then he pulled the djellaba up around his middle and came through the shed to the door. He stood there looking at all the water outside. And he looked inside into the corner and saw the donkey standing in the water. The water was moving over the tops of the planks, and I was still crouching there.

When it was time for breakfast, they found everything under the water. The tea, the sugar, the dishes, and the charcoal and wood too.

My mother said to her husband: "If we leave that boy there in the water, he's going to die."

"I'll go out and call an ambulance," he said. "It can take him to the hospital. Then we'll see what we're going to do."

"But it's still early," said my mother. "You can't telephone until the bacal opens."

We stayed a little longer that way, and then he went out to the bacal and called the ambulance, and it came. Two men were in it. They lifted me onto a stretcher and carried me outside. Then they put me into the ambulance. When I was inside it, I cried: "Thanks to Allah! Thanks to Allah! It's better to be sick in a bed than sick under the water!"

They drove me to the hospital and the doctor looked at me.

"Put him downstairs," he said.

They put me into a room with a lot of others. I stayed in bed there. When it was night, the doctor came downstairs and began to walk from one bed to another, looking at the people, and giving them whatever they needed. And he put two needles into me and went upstairs again.

And I stayed there. In the morning my head did not hurt anymore. But I could not stand up. They brought us all coffee, without bread or anything. At noon they brought lunch, and I ate. When night came, the doctor came with medicine and gave it again to everyone. And he put another needle inside me. Then I could sit up a little and talk to the others. I could even put my feet onto the floor. And when I found I could do that, I got up and began to walk around. If somebody needed something, I could get it and take it to his bed. I began to carry the bedpans and bottles around the room. And if somebody wanted water, I got it and took it to him.

And I stayed there fifteen days. All that time nobody came to see me, neither my mother nor my brother. No one. When it was visiting time many people came to see the men who were sick.

Why doesn't anybody come to see me? I was thinking. They would all be talking to their families, and eating the food their families had brought them. And I was just sitting on my bed looking at all the others.

I put my head under the covers and cried. Look! Everybody has someone to come and see him. And I have no one.

It was Thursday. The visitors all began to go out. Then I saw my mother coming in. The doctor was there, and he told me: "Today you're leaving."

"Ouakha."

My mother did not see me. I began to call out:

"Here I am!"

She came over and sat down on my bed. I kissed her hand.

"Why didn't you come to see me before?" I asked her. "All the others had people coming to see them. You never even came once."

"We didn't have time," she said.

"I see."

She had brought me a pot of tea and a few oranges and some biscuits.

"Here's the teapot," she told me. "I'm going to leave it with you until Sunday, and then I'll come back."

"No. I'm getting out today. Leave it here. And in the afternoon the man who gives our clothes back to us will come, and I'll bring the teapot back home with me. You have to go now."

"Ouakha," she said.

She went away, and I poured half a glass of tea and drank it. All the visitors were gone.

It was four o'clock. The man who gave back our clothes came around. He called my name.

I answered.

"Come on. Go upstairs. You're leaving."

There was an old man in the bed next to mine. He asked me: "Where are you taking that pot full of tea?"

"I'm carrying it back home," I told him.

"Will you sell me the tea in it?"

"Yes," I said.

"I'll give you two bilyoun for it."

"Ouakha."

I took the pot and poured the tea out of it into a bowl. And the old man handed me two bilyoun.

I had the teapot and the two bilyoun in my hand, and I went upstairs. And they gave me my clothes. I put them on and went out of the hospital. I walked past Dar Menebbhi, and down the Aqaba di Kasbah, past the cinema. Then I thought: Ah, what's this? A theatre?

I asked the man in the street: "How much does it cost to go into the cinema?"

"Two bilyoun," he told me.

Yes, I said to myself. The two bilyoun I got for the tea. I'll spend them and go inside and see what's in there. Then afterward I'll go home.

I bought a ticket at the window and went in. That was the first time I had been inside a cinema.

Now I see why people like to live in the city. This theatre is very fine, I thought. There were pictures of war, and there were airplanes flying.

When I came out it was night. Now I've got to go alone all the way to the Monopolio, and it's dark. I'll ask some boy if he's going out that way, and if he is I'll go with him.

I stopped a boy and said to him: "Are you going out to the tobacco factory?"

"No," he said. "I'm not."

I asked another, and he said no. I kept on asking, and a man going past heard me.

"Ha!" he said. "Boy! You want to go to the tobacco factory?"

"Yes," I told him. "If you're going, Sidi, please let me walk with you."

"Where do you live?" he said.

"In the orchard near the bacal."

"Let's go."

We walked until we came to the park at Bou Khach Khach. I said to him: "Now I know the way."

But he walked with me until we came to our house. Then I said: "This is where I live. Good-bye." And he went on.

I went to the house and knocked on the door. My mother opened it. "Ah! You've come!" she said. "Are you all right?"

"Yes, thanks to Allah."

"Are you strong now?"

"Yes, I'm strong."

I walked inside where her husband was, and kissed his hand. "Are you well?" he said.

"Yes." Then I asked my mother: "And the donkey? Where is he?"

"We've had bad luck," she told me. "He's dead."

"He died? Wasn't he sick first?"

"He stayed six days in the water, and he had nothing to eat, and then he died," she said.

"The poor donkey. If I'd stayed here I'd have died like him, in the water."

Dinner was ready, and we ate it. Afterward I went to the shed and lay down on my mat the same as always. There was no more water there now. It was outside in the orchard, but not in the house. And I slept.

In the morning while I was still sleeping, my mother's husband came and woke me up.

"What! Haven't you gone to work yet?" he said.

"I just came from the hospital. Tomorrow I will go to work."

"Yes, I know you. You want to play all day. You don't like pulling in the nets."

"Yes, I do. But now it's too late to go to work. This isn't the hour to go. Tomorrow I'll go."

"All right," he said.

We ate our breakfast. Then I said to Mohammed: "Do you know where we're going today? To the garbage dump. We'll find some old pieces of metal and take them and sell them. Then we can go to the cinema."

"Is the cinema a good place?" he said.

"Yes," I told him. "I went in yesterday and saw it."

"Let's go to the garbage dump."

I took a big, round basket and went out ahead of him. Walking, walking, the two of us, until we got to the bridge behind the Charf. We found a lot of boys there, looking for things in the garbage. Some had hoes, and some had pieces of wood or metal to dig into the garbage. It was all mixed, food and papers and rubbish. I looked for a while, and I found a metal tube. I bent it, and began to use it to dig with. The trucks kept coming to dump more things, and Mohammed and I kept digging. We filled the basket with pieces of metal. Then we found a piece of rope and tied it around the basket. There was a Jew who lived near the bull-ring, and he always bought everything I took him. Usually I sold him bones. He paid three gordas a kilo for them.

When I lifted the basket onto my shoulder, it was very heavy.

Mohammed said: "Let's carry it between us."

"No. You can't," I told him.

I carried the basket to the Jew. He weighed it and paid us twelve pesetas.

"See how much money there is here, Mohammed! We can go to the cinema as many times as we like!"

"Let's go now," he said.

"And the basket? Where are we going to leave it?"

"We can take it with us into the cinema."

"Ouakha. Come on," I said.

We started walking into the city. When we got to the cinema there were hundreds of boys standing around the ticket window, trying to buy tickets.

"Here. Take the basket," I told Mohammed. "I'm going to push in with those boys and buy the tickets."

I went into the crowd and began to push the same as the rest. After half an hour or more I got to the window and bought the tickets.

We went in at five o'clock and saw horses running. When we came out it was seven o'clock, and it was almost dark.

We went back home, and found my mother's husband there. He looked at me and said: "Where have you been?"

"We were out setting traps for birds, that's all," I told him.

"And the basket? What were you doing with that?"

"I took it with me in case I went by the beach and pulled a little on the nets. I thought they might give me a few fish."

Then he asked Mohammed: "Where have you been all day?"

"Looking for birds."

He gave him a slap in the face. "Tell me where you were all day. And why you came back so late."

"Just looking for birds," said Mohammed.

He slapped him harder. "Tell me the truth!"

"We were looking for pieces of metal, and we found some and sold them," said Mohammed. "And then we went to the cinema."

"Yes," my mother's husband said to me. "Now you're teaching my son to go to the cinema, and at his age."

"I didn't make him go. He wanted to go with me."

And he took a cane and began to hit my head with it. My mother came in and tried to stop him. "Please, Si Abdallah," she was saying. "Stop!"

"Take your hands off me!" I shouted. "You're the one who teaches him to do all these things."

He went on beating me on my face and hands, and I was crying. When he stopped, I cried a while and was quiet.

Then he said: "If you brought something to eat, eat it. There's nothing here for you."

"Ouakha," I said. "I don't have to eat tonight."

Later my mother came out with a little food. "Here, take this." I took it to my corner in the shed and ate it. I set the plate on the floor beside me and went to sleep.

In the morning I got up and went to the kitchen to get a piece of bread. The others were still asleep. There was no bread. So I went to the beach to work without bread. And the fishermen began to come along the beach. They stood around until the chief came. We put the ropes and oars and nets into the boat and pushed it out into the water. We pulled the net in three times. The fourth time the chief said: "That's enough."

It was late in the afternoon then. We carried the nets up into the dunes and left them there with the guard. And we went to the chief's shack, and he paid us each three rials.

I said to myself: "Ah! Three rials from the chief! Working all day without anything to eat, and I'm almost dead of hunger. I have money now. I'm going to eat. What's left I'll take home."

I went to the bacal and bought half a loaf of bread and a can of tuna fish and two oranges. Then I went and sat in the shade of the cactus bushes on the other side of the road, and ate everything. I had two rials left.

I went home. Only my mother was there.

"Well, aoulidi! Perhaps you worked today?"

"Yes. I worked."

"How much did they give you?"

"Two rials."

"Is that all?"

She took the money from me and left it on the table. Soon her husband came in.

"Well, young man, did you work today?"

"Yes."

"How much did you bring back?"

"Two rials."

"What? They gave you only two rials?"

"That's right."

"Or did you buy something to eat?" he said.

"No. I didn't eat anything."

Later my mother brought me a piece of bread. "Here," she said. "You've been all day without eating."

"Yes," I said. "Give it to me."

I took the piece of bread to my corner in the shed and ate it. Then I stayed there until my mother had made dinner.

"Come and eat," she said.

We ate, and then I went to sleep.

The next day when I woke up my head ached. I said to my mother: "I don't think I can go to work today. I feel sick."

"Aoulidi," she said. "Go, or else your stepfather is going to yell at you."

"Ouakha, I'll go, and if I can pull on the net I will. If I can't, I'll come back home."

I went out of the house that morning with a heavy pain in my head. I walked very slowly, I felt so sick.

I was walking along the road, and I came to the wall where people threw garbage. It stayed there until the trucks came to get it. There was a a lot of it lying there, in front of a place where there were two cafés. I stopped walking. Then I took a piece of wood and began to dig into the garbage. Digging, digging, and soon I saw a piece of paper. I said to myself: That looks like a peseta. In those days they had one-peseta notes printed brown. I picked it up and unfolded it.

Ah, it's a rial, I thought, not a peseta. I unfolded it all the way, and then I knew it was five rials.

By Allah, this is a fine day! Five rials, and I'm sick. Now I'll give this to my mother's husband, and he'll let me rest today.

I put the five-rial note into my pocket and went back home,

walking slowly because of the pain in my head.

When I went into the house, my mother said: "Ah, aoulidi! You've come back! You weren't able to work?"

"I don't feel well, no," I said. "But I found these five rials in the garbage."

Her husband heard me and said: "Let me see them."

"Here they are."

He took the money and put it in his pocket.

"Go on, go on," he said. "Go to the beach and work now. There's nothing the matter with you at all. You think five rials is a lot of money?"

"I know it's not such a lot," I said. "But if I'd gone and worked all day long, I sstill wouldn't have earned that much. I feel sick, and I found five rials, and so why do I have to go to the beach and work? I can go tomorrow."

"I told you to go now," he said. "Not tomorrow."

I went out. I was thinking: I'll work. But the money I earn I'll spend for food, and I won't go back home at all. I can eat here on the beach. And I was thinking that it would be better for me to sleep in one of the boats than live there in the house.

I came to the place where the nets were. I worked all day. My head kept hurting and I was dizzy. I could not pull very hard. In the afternoon the chief paid us. He gave each one two rials and a half.

This is very good, I thought. I took the money and went to a café there on the road. I sat down on the mat and said to the qahouaji: "Make me a glass of tea."

When I had the tea I began to eat. I finished eating and paid the qahouaji and went out.

Now where am I going to go? I thought. I don't know. I'll go back into the café and wait until it's dark. Then I'll go down to the beach and find a boat and sleep in it.

I sat there in the café until night came. I went down onto the beach in the dark. I looked around until I found a boat with a net in it. I lifted up the net and lay on the floor of the boat. Then I covered myself with the net. It was dry, and it was a good blanket. I went to sleep until morning.

And in the morning I did not wake up until a man came to take the net out of the boat.

"Who's this sleeping here?" he said.

"Good morning," I said to him.

"You stayed here all night?"

"Yes, I slept here."

"Weren't you cold?"

"No, I wasn't cold."

"Why didn't you go home to bed?"

"I didn't go," I said. "That's all."

After that I lived on the beach. Today and tomorrow, the time went by.

Chapter Two

Inch'allah

One night I wanted to go fishing. I picked up my fishing pole and my bag, went down to the river and dug for worms. I gathered some worms and fished there for a while. Then a gentleman came to me and asked me, "Do you want to work?"

I said yes. "What kind of work is it?"

He said, "There's a ship coming soon. It's loaded with cigarettes and we want to unload the cigarettes onto shore. If you want to work, you will get paid well."

I said, "Ouakha, I would like to work. I would like to work if there is any work."

He said, "Ouakha, come along."

I asked him where it was.

He said, "Do you see that light?"

I said, "Yes."

He said, "That's the place where you are going to work."

I asked him, "Is it just you and me? Are there other people?"

He said, "Yes. There are five other men besides us."

I told him, "Ouakha, I'm going to pick up my things first. Let's go."

We walked towards the light. We walked to a point on the beach where we could see the light in the water. We found other men waiting. We said Ahilan. The man who wanted me to work told them that he found me, I was going to work with them, I was

35

all right. One of them asked my name.

"My name is Larbi Ben Layachi."

I asked him his name.

"My name is Driss."

"Do you do this kind of work all the time?"

He said, "No, only now and then."

I asked him, "Where do all these men come from, do you know?"

He said, "The man who is in charge finds us."

The man in charge said, "Listen, this work is very dangerous. We cannot afford to give it more than thirty minutes."

He said, "Now, this is what I want you all to do. When the rowboat gets to shore, we have to start taking the boxes from the rowboat to the shore very fast. We have to put all the boxes on shore and when the truck gets here we are going to load it."

Then he took a flashlight out of his pocket and signaled the ship three times.

We waited a while until the rowboat came in. Then we took one box apiece and put them ashore until we emptied the rowboat. Then the rowboat went back to the big ship to get another load. The rowboat went back and forth until all the cigarettes were off the big ship. About a hundred and fifty cases. A few minutes later a truck came. We loaded all the cigarettes in the truck. When the truck was loaded, I asked the man in charge, "Who do these cigarettes belong to?"

He said, "To the man who has the bacal in Old Tangier."

"Does the man who owns the bacal in Old Tangier sell cigarettes on the black market?"

He said, "Don't you know?"

I said, "I don't know."

He said, "There are a lot of people who sell cigarettes on the black market. That's the way they make money, selling cigarettes.

It's against the law, everybody knows that."

I told him, "We have all done something against the law. haven't we?"

He said, "Sure. Jobs against the law always pay better money. For instance, look at you now. You could stay here fishing at this river for months and you wouldn't be able to make as much money as you made tonight. The man who owns the bacal pays everybody fairly."

I said, "It's good. Ouakha, when am I going to get paid?"

He said, "Tomorrow at noon come to Socco Chico."

I said, "Who should I look for to pay me?"

He said, "You'll look for me. You'll remember me."

I said, "Ouakha."

They all got into the truck and drove away.

I went back to the river and started to fish. I said to myself: Allah, I am very lucky tonight. I am going to make at least five thousand francs. Tonight must be my lucky night. I stayed there fishing. A little while later I heard noises like a machine. The machine was a police jeep. I stood watching the headlights for a while. They didn't seem to stop. Then the police turned the lights toward me and I was the only person in the river. They came straight to me. "What are you doing here?"

I told them, "As you can see, I am fishing."

One said, "Did you see anyone around here?"

I said, "I didn't see anyone. You people are here now. That's all I saw."

He said, "I am talking to you, and you are raising your hands at me." He said, "What's the matter with you? Aren't you happy that we're asking you these questions?"

"Sir, may Allah bless you. You ask me if I saw anyone and I told you I didn't. All I saw were you people."

A commissaire came out of the jeep. He slapped me, and said,

"Ouakha, come here."

I picked up my fishing equipment. They put me in the jeep with them and took me away. They took me to the commissariat in Malabata. It was about three-thirty in the morning. The inspector who had slapped me took my fishing pole and broke it. He took my can of fish and threw it away, and he slapped me twice. One policeman took me to a room, locked me in. I said to myself, Allah, it looks like it's a very lucky night for me. Well, what am I going to do now? If I tell them the truth, they would probably never find the people who took the cigarettes out. If I lie to them, they're not going to believe me. Please, Allah, help me.

A policeman came and opened the door. He said, "Come out." He took a pack of cigarettes out of his pocket.

The same commissaire said, "Do you smoke?"

I said, "Yes."

He gave me a cigarette and said, "Here, enjoy yourself. Let me give you a light." He lit my cigarette and said, "Listen very carefully to what I am saying. I am going to ask you something, and you've got to tell me the truth. You're not going to lie to me."

"Ouakha, if I know anything, I'll tell you."

He said, "Good. Who came close to you where you were fishing?"

I said, "I didn't see anyone. If I saw anyone, I would have told you before you brought me here, when I was still at the river." He hit me a couple of times. Blood started running from my nose.

I told him, "You have no right to do this to me."

He called a policeman named Charhadi. Charhadi said, "Yes?" The commissaire told him, "Come over here."

Charhadi came to me and said, "Take your clothes off."

I said, "Why should I take my clothes off? Look, I didn't do anything. You're just taking advantage of me. This is not right."

He kicked me in my stomach and I fell to the floor. Another

policeman came and the two of them picked me up. The commissaire said, "Hit him." They started hitting me. They hit me and hit me, again and again.

The commissaire said, "Okay, that's enough." He came close to me and said, "Now what do you think? Are you going to tell us the truth? Did you see anybody take cigarettes, or didn't you?"

I said, "No, I didn't see anyone. I can't tell you anything. I didn't see anyone. If I did see anyone, I would have told you. I would have nothing to lose. I would have told you the truck came, they loaded the cigarettes and left. That's all I am going to say to you. Now look what you did to me."

The commissaire said, "Hit him again."

They began to hit me again, until I could no longer scream. The next morning, when I woke up, I couldn't move. I couldn't do anything. The policemen that were there left, and a different group came in. They came in and opened the door. Another commissaire came in.

He said to me, "What's the matter with you? You are so stubborn. Why don't you want to say who took the cigarettes?"

I told him, "I didn't see anything. If I had I would have told the commissaire last night."

He said, "You are a liar, you donkey. Those people were very near you."

I said, "If I had seen anything, I would have told the other commissaire. Now look what's happened to me. Why all this?"

He said, "Quiet, you dog." He slapped me twice. It was impossible to talk to those people. It was about nine o'clock. They brought me a loaf of bread and a can of tea. He said, "Here, have your breakfast."

He said, "Do you smoke?"

I said, "Yes, I do."

I told him, "This is the same story as last night. The commissaire gave me one cigarette and look what happened to me."

Then he told me, "You don't have to be afraid. I am not like the other commissaire."

He said, "Here, smoke."

I started smoking the cigarette and drinking the tea. I couldn't eat the bread at all.

He said, "Now, what do you think? Are you going to tell us the truth, or are you not?"

I told him what I already had said: "I didn't see anything."

He said, "If you didn't see anything, and you won't tell us anything, you are going to jail."

I said, "I am already in jail. All night long a beating and now this morning you are doing the same thing." Then he kicked me right in the stomach.

I fell down and he said, "Bring him out." They took me out and started hitting me again. He said, "Ouakha, now you are going to tell us the truth."

I told him again, "I didn't see anything. There is no one to punish you. I believe you will all be punished by Allah."

I said, "The judgment day will come and you will be judged by him like you are judging me now. He's the one who is going to get justice. You people do whatever you please. You can't kill me, if Allah doesn't kill me."

He said, "Yes, there is someone who will judge us."

I said, "No, there isn't. Look what you did to me. There is no one I can tell about what you've done. Who's in charge of you people?"

He said, "You wait a minute. I am going to show you who's in charge of us."

He took a bucket full of water and poured it on top of me. Then I was really cold. The room was freezing. There were no blankets, there was nothing. I said to myself, Allah, you are watching everything. I am asking you to get me justice with these people. I have nobody else to complain to except you.

I said, "Allah, what a day this is."

Then the man said, "Sit down." He gave me a cigarette and said, "Here, smoke." He said, "Are you going to tell the truth now?"

"I already told you the truth. If you want me to lie to you, I will."

He said, "Take him back again." They took me back to the same room and locked me in. I hated that room. What could I do? I didn't have any choice at all. Allah, I thought, please make the best out of this situation. I stayed there all day long. It was already dark.

Late at night another policeman came and opened the door. He said, "Come out." I came out.

He said, "Now what do you think? Did you see anyone taking the cigarettes, or didn't you?"

"No, I didn't see anybody. I've been telling you the same thing all the time. You are not listening, I guess. Now I am not going to talk anymore. You do whatever you want."

He said, "Hit him again." They hit me and hit me again. I didn't say anything. He said, "That's enough." They picked me up and took me back to the room and locked the door.

In the morning the commissaire came, the same man who had picked me up from the river. He said, "Are you going to tell us the truth?"

I said, "What truth am I going to tell you? You see how I look and you ask me to tell the truth. You must be out of your mind. Now, it doesn't really matter. You are not going to hear another word from me."

He slapped me.

Then they brought my breakfast. A loaf of bread and a can of tea. I drank the tea. I couldn't eat any bread.

He said, "Sit down."

He was typing on the typewriter. He asked me, "What is your name?"

"My name is Ben Layachi."

"Where were you born?"

"In Tangier."

"Do you have anybody here?"

"Yes, my mother, my brothers and everybody."

"Where do you live?"

"Near the tobacco factory."

"What neighborhood?"

"Near the beach in Monopolio."

"How old are you?"

"Eighteen."

"Are you married?"

"No."

He was typing everything on the machine. He took the paper out and said, "Sign here." He said, "Now you are going to go to the tribunal." He said, "Get him out." They took me back to the room. About twelve-thirty the police wagon came. They put me in and drove to the tribunal. They took me to the judge who hears such cases.

The judge said, "Ahilan. Did you tell the truth to the police?"

He said, "Here in your file, the police are saying you helped some people smuggle cigarettes and you didn't want to tell the truth about it. How much money did they give you?"

I told him, "Are these the first words you are going to say to me—how much money did I get? You are not going to ask me how I feel or what they did to me?"

He said, "All that is nothing. You will go to jail. There is a doctor and he will take care of you."

I told him, "Thank you very much, Your Honor; that's very kind of you."

He said, "Now, are you going to tell me the truth? I'll let you go right now."

I told him, "What kind of truth can I tell you now? If I did see anything, I would have told them a long time before all this happened to me."

He said, "All you boys are very stubborn." He wrote something on a piece of paper and gave it to the policeman. He said, "Take him." They put me back in the wagon. They took me to the Casbah jail. There they gave my paper to the guard. He searched me and didn't find anything. He opened the door and said, "Get in."

In the jail I found one man I recognized. He said, "Ahilan, Layachi, what's the matter? What happened?"

"It was my lucky night, that's why I'm here. If you look for trouble, you really find it, and trouble always follows you. I didn't look for trouble, trouble looked for me. On Thursday night I was fishing in the river. The police came and said, Come with us. That's what happened. I went with them. They told me I saw some people taking cigarettes from a ship."

He said, "Ah, this is terrible. It's a shame." He took me and made a place for me and gave me two blankets.

I told him, "I'm very cold."

He went to other prisoners to ask if anyone had an extra blanket. "That boy who came today is very cold and they beat him so badly he can't even move. Please, if anybody has any extra blankets . . ."

He brought them to me. I laid two blankets on top of the mat and went to sleep.

I slept until the next morning with no trouble. When I woke the next morning, I asked my friend, Mimun, if he had any cigarettes.

He went to his place and brought me a pack of cigarettes. I smoked one cigarette and I felt better. Then I began to remember.

I said to myself, Why did I get myself into trouble? Trouble is looking for me and I don't know what to do about it.

Other prisoners came to me and asked, "What did you do? Why did they beat you?"

I said, "Don't you know how the police are? I don't have to tell you the story."

One of the prisoners said, "These police have nobody to judge them, even if it's they who break the rules. On the other hand, I believe if you break the rules, you get punished."

I started thinking to myself. I said to myself, This is very good pay. I was going to get paid. The man told me I would be paid well. I am like a donkey. I went through all that trouble taking the cigarettes out and all that beating and Allah knows what's going to happen.

About ten o'clock the doctor came and said, "Bring out all the sick people."

They began to take sick people out one by one.

They told the doctor, "There is a boy here who they brought yesterday."

Two men came and picked me up between them. They took me out to see him.

The doctor looked at me and asked me, "What happened? Why did this happen to you?"

I told him, "Well, Doctor, I guess I'm very lucky. Bad things happen to lucky people. When accidents happen, they happen. It is Allah's will."

He said, "Yes. This is not bad; it will go away." He gave me some aspirin to take and a shot. He said, "Take him." They took me back to my place.

I sat there. When it was time to eat, they would bring my food to my place. I spent about ten days there and one morning they put me in a wagon and took me down to the tribunal.

The judge called my name and said, "Stand up."

I stood up.

He asked me, "Did you see anybody take the cigarettes from the ship?"

I said, "No, Your Honor,"

He said, "Your papers say you saw some people take cigarettes out of a ship, and didn't tell the truth to the police."

I said, "Your Honor, please. If I did see something, I would tell. I don't have anything to hide. They beat me for three days in the commissariat. For ten days I've been in jail without a reason. I didn't do anything."

He said, "If you had told the police the truth, this wouldn't have happened to you. Now, what do you say? Did you see anyone take the cigarettes, or didn't you?"

I said, "No, I didn't. I was fishing at the river. When the police came, they took me to the commissariat. The commissaire took my fishing pole and broke it and threw away my can full of fish, and I didn't know why. He asked me if I saw anybody take cigarettes off a ship. I said I didn't."

He said, "That's all."

Then I said, "Is it right for the police to do whatever they want? Nobody says anything. Nobody makes them prove that what they say is true. Nobody does anything."

He said, "Enough! Sit down!"

A policeman took me back to the bench. I sat down. The four judges began to talk together. I couldn't hear what they were saying. In a few minutes the judge called, "Ben Layachi."

I said, "Yes, sir."

"Stand up! The tribunal sentences you to one month of jail. The next time you see something you must tell the police. The next time the police find you down there fishing at two-thirty in the morning, we are going to sentence you to one year in jail. Now the tribunal sentences you to one month in jail."

I said, "Thank you, Your Honor. All the trouble I went through, a beating and three days at the commissariat, and now you are telling me I can't go back to the river and fish at night."

He said, "That's enough! Out!"

Then two policemen dragged me downstairs to the room and said, "Stay here." There was another policeman by the door watching. I stayed in the room until they finished sentencing all the prisoners. Each one had a different case. Some of them stole. Others fought. When they finished the sentencing, the wagon came. They put us all into the wagon and took us back to the jail, where prisoners began to ask, "How much did you get? And how much did you get?"

My friend, Mimun, said, "How about you, Layachi? How much did you get?"

I told him, "One month."

He said, "One month is nothing."

I said, "Sure, one month is nothing."

He said, "You are very lucky. There are a lot of people here who get six or seven months or a year for nothing."

I said, "This month is a gift to the man who owns the cigarettes."

He said, "Tell me the truth, did you really help unload those cigarettes?"

"Sure I did," I said. "The man got his cigarettes, and now I'm in trouble. What do I do?"

He said, "Well, you wait until you get out of jail. Then go see the man who took the cigarettes. Tell him the story, exactly what happened."

I said, "Do you think he will believe me?"

Mimun said, "Yes, he probably already knows."

We continued talking for a while.

Then soup came.

Mimun said, "Everybody get into line."

The soup was like water with a few vegetables. It tasted good. It was warm. Everybody took their soup and we started eating. We stayed there talking.

About three-thirty they opened the door and said, "Everybody out to the patio." We walked upstairs to the patio and there I met a man named Ahmed. I asked him why he was in jail.

He said, "I beat up a policeman."

I said, "Why?"

He said, "The policeman promised to marry my daughter. When he got her pregnant, he didn't want to see her anymore."

I said, "How long have you been here?"

He said, "Three months."

I said, "Have you been sentenced yet?"

He said, "Yes, they gave me six months."

I said, "What happened to the policeman?"

He said, "They kicked him out. He is no longer a policeman."

I said, "What is your daughter going to do now?"

He said, "Well, she'll stay home until she has the baby. Then she will either get married or go to work."

I said, "Aren't you glad they kicked out the policeman?"

He said, "That policeman is a no good dog. He deserved it."

Then Mimun called me to play soccer.

I told Ahmed, "Allah got you justice. Now, excuse me—I am going to play ball with these men."

We played ball for a while, then they called: *Okay, everybody downstairs.*

We went downstairs and everyone went back to his place. I sat and started thinking about my trouble. Allah forbids bad things and punishes people who do them. So here I am. I did something bad and I am getting punished for it. The one with bad things written in his head will suffer for them. I was fishing. If I had stayed fishing I would have made a little money. At least it would have been my own sweet money. It would have been a lot better than this evil money I was going to get. The evil man came and said, "Would you like to work?" The one who is not satisfied with a little, he wouldn't be satisfied with a lot. I didn't get paid anything. I didn't stay fishing. I didn't stay outside, and now I'm in jail. That's a great accomplishment. That's all the luck I had.

I stayed in my place until Mimun came. He said, "Layachi, you shouldn't worry too much about this. You have served eleven days; you have nineteen days left. That's not a long time to go. You'll be out of here before you know it. Try to relax now. Let's play parcheesi."

I said, "Oh, yes, sure, sure."

He said, "No, come on, come on. It will pass the time. It is better than just sitting here and worrying."

I went with him and we started playing parcheesi with two other prisoners. We stayed playing until they knocked on the door and said, *Soup!*

My friend, Mimun, said, "Okay, everybody get in line."

Mimun began to divide the soup. I took my soup and went back to my place. I ate my soup and took my dish to wash it. I stayed there today and tomorrow, today and tomorrow, until I had finished out the month.

One morning they called me: "Layachi, get your clothes; you are going home." I gathered my things and said to my friend Mimun, "Allah ihennik," and I stepped out the door.

They asked me if I had any money.

I said, "No." They asked me to sign a paper and I did.

A guard said, "Allah ihennik. You are free."

I walked out of the jail door, and felt like I had never been inside. It was a beautiful day and the sun was shining. I said to myself, I think I am going to go down to the beach and have myself a good swim. Then I'll go and see the man who owns the bacal.

I walked down the Casbah through the narrow streets until I got to the seafront. I went right to the beach. I took my clothes off and left my shorts on and started swimming. The water felt so good. I swam for a long time. When I got out of the water I went to the warm sand. I stayed there for a while, then got dressed.

I started walking towards Old Tangier. I walked until I reached Tanja el Bali. I crossed the river where I had been fishing. I said, Oh, yes, this is the place where I was picked up and taken to the commissariat. That's my gift to the man who got the cigarettes.

I walked uphill. I came to a shepherd and asked him if he knew of a bacal that sold cigarettes around there.

He said, "Yes. Do you see that bacal way down there? That's the place where they sell cigarettes."

I walked to the bacal, went in, and said, "Salaam aleikoum," and the man there said, "Aleikoum salaam."

He said, "Aoulidi, do you need anything?"

I said, "Yes, I do, I need to tell you a story and I hope you will believe me."

He said, "Aoulidi, if you tell the truth, I will believe you."

I told him, "Sidi, about a month ago I took some cigarettes out of a ship at night with some men down at the beach. The man who was in charge told me to come the next day to the Socco Chico and he would pay me. We loaded the cigarettes on the truck. The truck left and I went back to fishing. Later the police came and they took me. They broke my fishing pole and threw my can of fish away. They took me to the commissariat and beat me for three days. Then they took me to the tribunal and I was given one month of jail. I just got out today. Now, I am broke and I would like you to give me what is coming to me."

He said, "Those weren't my cigarettes."

I said, "They were. Because I asked the man in charge there who the cigarettes belonged to. He told me they were yours. Is there anybody else who sells cigarettes in Tanja el Bali?"

He said, "No, I am the only one here who has a cigarette license."

I said, "Well, if you want the truth, the cigarettes were yours. Have you paid everybody?"

He said, "Yes, I remember, I paid five people. And the man in charge did tell me that the next day one boy didn't show up for his money. I understand now. Ouakha, all right." He took five thousand francs and gave it to me. He took ten thousand francs and said, "This is for the sacrifice you made. Now, you go on and don't say anything to anybody."

I said, "No, sir, if I was going to say anything I would have told the police." I said Allah ihennik.

I put the money in my pocket and said to myself, I think the trouble about the cigarettes was worth it. I'll buy two cartons of cigarettes for my friend, Mimun, and go to see him. He was very nice to me.

I walked down to the road, to the bus stop, and waited for the bus. The bus came, and I got on it. The man who charges the fares said, "Please, pay twenty francs."

I gave him five thousand francs. He said, "Don't you have anything smaller than this?"

I said, "I don't."

He said, "I just saw you putting money back in your pocket."

I said, "I don't have anything smaller in my pocket."

I showed him the ten-thousand-franc note. He said, "What did you do, rob somebody or something?"

I told him, "That's none of your business. Your business is to charge a fare."

He said, "What's the matter with you? You're a fanatic."

I said, "I'm not a fanatic. You're the one who started all this."

He said, "I don't have change for five thousand francs."

I told him, "Give me back my five thousand francs when we get to Socco. I will get change and pay you."

He said, "I'm not going to give you five thousand francs. You might run away with my twenty francs."

I said, "How could I run away with your twenty francs? I'm on bus! Don't you trust me?"

"I'm not going to trust you because this is not my money. This money belongs to the bus company." I asked the people who were riding the bus if they had twenty francs. I said, "When we get to Socco, I will pay you back."

One old man took twenty francs and gave them to me. I took the twenty francs and gave them to the man who charges fares. He gave me back my five thousand francs. I sat down. We reached Socco. I got off the bus and told the man who gave me twenty francs to come with me to a bacal. I went to the bacal and bought two cartons of cigarettes for two thousand francs. I gave the man back his twenty francs. I walked up to the Casbah to take the cigarettes to my friend. I went to the office and asked to see him.

He said, "What is your friend's name?"

"Mimun."

He said, "Oh, the head prisoner."

"Yes."

The guard said, "Ouakha, come with me." We went inside and opened the gate. He called my friend, Mimun. Mimun came out.

"Oh," he said, "it is you, Layachi." I said, "Yes." He said, "What happened?"

I told him, "I went to the man at the bacal. He paid me, so I bought you some cigarettes." We talked for a while. The guard said, "Okay, your time is up."

I told Mimun, "If things work out all right for me, I'll come and see you from time to time."

He said, "Well, you don't have to worry about it. If you can come or if you can't, don't worry."

I said Allah ihennik.

I left the jail and walked down to Socco.

I said, Now, what am I going to do? I think I'm going to eat. I went to a restaurant. I ate a good meal. I had a glass of tea.

I thought, Now, where am I going to go? I think I'm going to go to the Socco Chico to Layachi's Café. I'll sleep there until morning. I went down to Layachi's Café. I asked the qahouaji for a glass of tea. I stayed there drinking my tea. Another boy who worked there asked me if I wanted to play a hand of cards.

I said, "Ouakha." We played cards for a while.

He said, "Now I'm very tired. I'm going to sleep."

I asked him, "Where do you sleep?"

He said, "I sleep up there on that mat."

I asked him, "Is it all right if I sleep there?"

He said, "Of course. You bought a glass of tea." He went to the mat to sleep. I followed him and lay next to him in a corner and went to sleep.

Chapter Three

True Love

In the morning I went down to the train station to see if I could find anyone who needed help with their suitcases. I stayed there for a long time and didn't find anyone to help. By then the sun was getting very hot.

I said to myself, I didn't find any work here. I think I'll go to swim. I walked to the beach, which was very close. I took off my clothes near the beach and started to swim. After swimming for a while, I lay on the sand.

As I way lying there, a beautiful Spanish girl came. She lay four or five yards away from me and I said, "Buenos días." She said, "Buenos días." I asked her, "Do you live around here?" She said, "We live over there in La Avenida de España. My parents have a restaurant here at the beach." I asked if they needed any help in the restaurant.

She said, "We do. You can work in the restaurant and earn your room and board, plus a small salary. We can't pay too much because we don't work all year round, only in the summer when we have good business."

I said, "Bueno. What is your name?"

"My name is María. What is your name?"

"Ben Layachi."

She said, "Do you have any family here?"

"I do—my mother, stepfather, and two brothers." She asked

where we lived. "Near the tobacco factory."

"Why don't you come along and meet my mother and father."

I told her, "Bueno." I picked up my clothes and we walked together to the café.

María told her father, "I found this man at the beach swimming. He asked me if we needed any help. I said I thought so, and I brought him to see you. I think he would be good."

Her father said to me, "What is your name?"

"Ben Layachi."

María's father asked me if I would like to work with them. I said yes. I asked him how much he was going to pay me.

He told me, "I will pay you three rials a day, your food, and we have a room for you to sleep in."

"Bueno. Do you want me to start today?"

"Yes, start today."

"What is my job?"

"Your job is to wake up early in the morning, sweep, take all the tables and chairs out to the terrace and get all the keys to the dressing rooms for the swimmers. When the people come, show them to their cabins. If anyone rents a dressing room, give him the key and show him his cabin."

"Bueno," I said.

María's mother came in and asked if I would like something to eat.

"Yes, I would."

She asked what I would like.

I told her, "Just a piece of bread with butter and café con leche."

She fixed this for me and gave it to me. "Here, eat," she said.

After I ate, I said to myself, Thanks to Allah I have found a job and with my meals, too. I stayed there, and soon people began to come down to the beach to swim. Some people came into the café and asked for dressing rooms. I gave the keys and showed people to the dressing rooms all day. Later I began to feel hungry. I went to the kitchen and I asked Señora Lola for something to eat.

She fixed me a plate with beef and green beans and gave me a half a loaf of bread and told me, "Eat now. Anytime you are hungry, ask me."

"Muchas gracias, Señora." I went out to the terrace. When I finished eating, I took the plate back to the kitchen. I asked Señor José if I could have a café con leche. I took the coffee to the terrace. I waited for any other people who might come to rent dressing rooms.

It started to get late, and the sun was beginning to set. María came out and said, "We have to take the tables and chairs inside now, you and I. It's time for us to close."

"You don't have to move the tables and chairs inside. This is my job," I said.

María told me, "It's all right. I just want to show you where to put them. I can help you for the first time. In the morning it will be easier for you because you can see how we do it now."

We took all the tables and chairs inside and she showed me where to put them. After we had brought them all in, she said to me, "Come with me now, Layachi, and I will show you your room where you will be sleeping." My room was next to the kitchen with one window which looked out towards the dressing rooms. Señora Lola showed me where my food was for my evening meal. "You may eat now—fish, eggs, bread, or anything," she said.

"Muchas gracias, Señora."

Señor José, Señora Lola, and María took their wraps. Señora Lola said, "Buenas noches, Layachi. We will see you in the morning."

"Buenas noches," I said, and they left. I decided to have a look around for myself and walked around the café. I went to the kitchen and made coffee. I ate at a table in the kitchen. After I finished eating I decided to go to sleep. I went to my room, which had a bed with two blankets and a small table in the corner. I said to myself, This is a beautiful place. I went to bed, and soon was asleep. I awoke just as the sun was coming up, dressed, and went to wash my face. It was warm already. What a glorious day!

I opened the doors and began to sweep out the kitchen and café. I also had to sweep off the terrace. I picked up the trash and put it in the can outside the back door of the kitchen and returned the broom to its place. I washed down the terrace with a hose in order to keep the dust down. When I finished, I started to take the tables outside. When all the tables were out, I placed the chairs around them. A little bit later Señor José, Señora Lola, and María arrived. They said, "Buenos días, Layachi."

"Buenos días."

They went to the kitchen with two big baskets full of supplies for the day. Señor José came to me and said, "You have done a good job this morning."

"Yes, gracias," I said, "that's what I'm here for, to work."

"We like people who like to work." Señor José went to the kitchen and they started preparing the food for the day.

Señora Lola asked me if I had eaten any breakfast and I told her no.

"I will make café for you first. I will fix some breakfast for you," she told me.

Señor José asked me to go to the bacal for salt and pepper which he had forgotten. "By the time you get back, your breakfast will be ready. Get one kilo of salt and one-quarter kilo of pepper." He gave me ten rials and I walked to the bacal, which was nearby. I asked for one kilo of salt and one-quarter kilo of pepper and gave the man at the counter ten rials. I took the change and my groceries and walked back to the café.

"Here is the salt and pepper, Señora Lola," and I gave them to her.

"Gracias, Layachi." She already had made coffee. She filled a glass with café con leche and gave me a plate with two pieces of bread and two eggs. "Here is your breakfast, Layachi. Come and eat." I took my plate and coffee and went to the terrace. María took a glass of café con leche and came to sit with me. María had beautiful long black hair and big blue eyes.

"María, are you going to swim today?"

She said, "Yes, when we finish everything for the day, I will go to swim. Are you going to swim with me?"

"Bueno."

We finished eating breakfast. I took the dishes back to the kitchen. They were fixing the food for the day. I asked if there was anything I could do to help.

Señora Lola said, "If you would like to wash up these pots and pans, it would be fine."

"Bueno," I said. I started washing the pots and pans. When I finished washing them, I hung up the pots on the hooks. I wiped the pans and put them together.

Señora Lola said, "We have finished this work. If you would like to go for a swim, go ahead."

"Yes, I'd like to go for a swim now."

María said, "Why don't you wait a minute. Don't think you're the only one going. I want to go, too."

"Bueno. If you want to go, let's go."

María went inside to her room. She changed to a bathing suit. We walked down to the water, and with her bathing suit on I saw how really beautiful she was. We jumped in and started swimming. I asked her if she was going to the plancha.

"Yes, what about you?"

"Sure, I'm going, too."

We climbed up onto the plancha and dove off into the water. We climbed back up in order to dive off again and did this many times. After a little while, some men came up to the plancha. I recognized one as a guard at the jail. His name was Omar.

He said, "Buenos días, María."

And she said, "Buenos días. Today, I see you came early."

"Yes, I did. Who is this swimming with you?"

"He is our employee, working for us," María told him.

Omar said, "He is only your employee and you are swimming with him? He isn't your kind. You shouldn't be swimming together."

María said, "Omar, stop talking like that. Don't you know he understands Spanish? He speaks Spanish."

"Bueno, bueno, I know you like poor men. But if I were you, I wouldn't speak to him even if he gave me a pile of money," Omar said.

María said to him, "Look, it's not a matter of money. The thing is for people to be kind to one another."

Omar said, "Maybe. But I think I saw this man in jail three or four days ago."

"I don't care, even if he was in jail; he can do anything he wants to. Our only interest in him is for him to work for us."

Omar said, "How could you give a job to a robber? All these poor men are only robbers. If you think I'm lying, wait, I'm going to ask him."

Omar came over and said Ahilan.

"What do you want?" I said.

"Come over here, closer," Omar said. "Were you in the jail a few days ago?"

"Yes," I said.

Omar said, "Are you the one who was in for black market tobacco?"

"Yes, I was."

"It doesn't matter. I just wanted to ask you, that's all," Omar said. "Can't you see, María? Do you think I'm lying to you? These poor men you can't trust. They're all a bunch of robbers."

María told him, "Stop it, stop it, I don't like what you say. I think it's best for you not to talk to me any more, Omar."

"Sure, I know you like him."

"I like all people, if they are good. I don't like selfish people like you. Look what kind of talking they do. What has the man done to you? Then you say they are no good. How can you say that?" María turned to me and said, "Layachi, let's leave. People will be coming soon and we have work to do."

We dove and swam out to the beach and went to lie down on the sand.

I asked María, "What was that guard Omar asking you?"

"He was just talking to himself. He always does that."

"It looks as if he likes you. That's why he is saying all those things to you."

She told me, "He's been coming here for a long time talking to me and I don't like him. He talks all the time with his filthy mouth. He is not good. I don't like anybody with a filthy mouth."

I told her, "María, you are a person who likes the truth; so I trust what you tell me."

We stayed there for a while together on the sand. María stood up and said, "Layachi, if you think you can run fast, why don't you try to catch me?"

"Bueno, why don't you run?"

She started running up the beach. I took off after her and caught her ankles to make her fall. We were on the sand, and I thought maybe she had something in mind. Maybe she wanted to do something with me. I said to myself, this is the second day I have been working. If something happens between us, perhaps her father wouldn't like it, and I might lose this job. María laughed and laughed. When she smiled, she looked lovely. In a few minutes her mother called us. She called, "María, María! Come!"

María told me, "Layachi, let's go. My mother is calling."

We ran all the way to the café and I went to shower. And María went to the ladies' shower, took a shower and dressed. When she came out the sunlight was falling on her long black hair which she was combing over her shoulder. I thought to myself, If any man on the beach sees María I know they will like her immediately. They cannot help it.

I went into the café to get the keys, and waited for people to come. Some people came to ask for dressing rooms. I took them to empty dressing rooms and gave them the keys. During the day, the café was full and busy all day long. Time passed quickly. When the people finished swimming and using the dressing room, they would bring the key to Señor José and pay him.

Around four-thirty in the afternoon Señora Lola called me. "Why don't you come to have something to eat now. You must be hungry."

"Yes, I am hungry."

She fixed tortillas with eggs and potatoes and gave them to me and asked me if I wanted something to drink.

"Yes, may I have a Coca-Cola?"

A few minutes later María came in to fry some pieces of fish, and she came to sit with me and eat at my table. "Layachi, what do you think? Is this work good? Do you like working for us?"

"Yes, it's good. If this job were steady, it would be very good for me."

"You don't have to worry now because it is summer and you are working for us. When the fall comes, we will pay you a little and you can look after the place. It will be like your home."

"I would like that."

María said to me, "Layachi, do you have any girlfriend?"
I told her, "No. We Muslims are not allowed to have girl-friends. We are only allowed to marry and have our wives."
Then I laughed. "Why are you asking me, María?"
"I am only asking you, that's all. Do you go to the cinema?"
I said, "Yes, I go once in a while."
"What do you think? Can we go this coming Sunday, you and I?"
"Yes, why not? If I don't go to the cinema with you, who would I go with? Would your father let you go to the cinema with me?"
"Yes, my father would let me. He wouldn't say anything."
"We should go."
Then she laughed and I looked at her. So pretty. I began to like her very much. When we had almost finished eating, Omar came into the café.
Señor José asked, "Omar, how are you? What would you like to drink?"
"I would like a beer."
Señor José gave him a beer. "Where did you find that man who is working for you, José?"
"I didn't find him. My daughter María met him while she was swimming."
Omar said, "Your daughter met him down on the beach and brought him and you gave him a job? Don't you think you should know something about him before he starts working for you?"
José told him, "We needed someone to work for us right away, and that's why we hired him. I think he is the right person to work with us."
Omar said, "Oh, but my friend, you don't know him. Don't you know he is a big robber, a criminal? It just so happens that

four or five days ago he got out of jail."

José asked, "What is this? Do you know why he was in jail?"

"They unloaded a ship full of black market tobacco. This is the only one they caught."

By this time María and I finished eating. We took the dishes back to the kitchen. María went out to sit in the sun. I said to myself: I have nothing to do. I will sit with María.

I lit up a cigarette and María and I started talking.

A few minutes later Señor José called me, "Layachi, Layachi."

"Yes, Señor José."

"I want to talk to you."

"Bueno, I am coming."

I went to him. "Señor José?"

He asked me, "Were you in jail?"

"Yes, I was in jail."

"Why? Did you steal anything?"

"No, I didn't steal anything. You see, what happened—I was fishing in the river at night. The police came to me. They told me I had helped some men unload a ship with tobacco. I told the police that I hadn't seen any tobacco and I hadn't unloaded any ship; I was only fishing. They took me away anyhow. That's what I went to jail for."

Omar said, "There, you see. I'm not lying."

Señor José asked me if I had ever gone to jail for stealing. I told him, no.

Señor José said, "All right, go on."

I went back to María. I told María, "This Omar is making too much of my going to jail. He went to your father and told him I went to jail for being a big thief."

María said, "Don't worry about it. He talks about everyone. You aren't the first one."

Omar came outside to sit at our table.

Omar asked María if she was going with him to the cinema on Sunday.

"No, on Sunday Layachi and I are going to the cinema."

"Oh, okay," Omar said and looked at me with a mean look in his eyes.

"María, if he wants to come to the cinema with us, he can. I don't mind," I said. "The cinema is for everyone, not just you and me."

María said, "I would like to go with just you."

"Okay. it's up to you," I said.

Omar was annoyed and got up to go back inside. He went to the bar and began talking to Señor José.

María asked me if I ever had gone to the cinema with a girl. I said no. I asked her if she liked me.

Then she laughed. She said, "I don't know exactly. I'm still thinking."

I said, "You are such a beautiful girl. I like you very much."

"Yes, I like you, too. Now that you are working for us, we should be friends and go to the cinema together."

"Yes, bueno," I told her.

We went inside to the kitchen and I told Señora Lola, "You have been working. You should sit down for a while. María and I will wash the dishes."

Señora Lola said, "Yes, Layachi, muchas gracias."

María and I began to wash and dry the dishes, talking and laughing. The work was beautiful and I liked it very much. When we finished washing the dishes, we dried them.

Later in the afternoon Señor José began to count the money from the day. When they were getting ready to leave, Señora Lola said, "Layachi, your dinner is here. Now we are going to go. Any time you want to eat, go ahead."

"Gracias, Señora Lola."

And Señor José said, "Now we are leaving. See you in the morning. Buenas noches."

I said, "Buenas noches."

And María told me, "Take care of yourself and eat well."

"Yes," I said. I thought to myself: I never had a job like this. I am very lucky.

María said, "Buenas noches," and they left. I began to bring all the tables and chairs back inside. Aftewards I went to the kitchen to make coffee and filled a glass with café con leche. I sat down and lit a cigarette and looked out over the sea. It was a beautiful, beautiful evening. I was so relaxed. I watched the waves breaking up on the beach. They made a beautiful sound. I gave thanks to Allah. I sat there smoking and watching the waves break. When it started getting dark I said to myself, I will eat dinner, then go to bed.

I went to the kitchen and brought out the food Señora Lola had left for me. I finished eating. I locked the windows and doors of the café. I went to my room and went to bed. I slept until early morning.

When I woke up, I swept and then took the water hose and washed down the terrace. I began to take out all the tables and chairs. I knew that it was going to be a good day. I prepared the café. A little while later they came in.

"Buenos días, Layachi."

"Buenos días," I said.

María stood close to me and asked, "Layachi, did you sleep well last night?"

"Yes, I had a good night's sleep. And you?"

"I did, too. I slept quite well," María said.

She laughed. Señora Lola made coffee. She filled a glass for me. She told me, "Layachi, now you are like our son. You don't have to wait for me. You can make anything for yourself that you like."

Soon María filled a glass with coffee and came out to where I was sitting. She asked me, "What do you think of this day?"

"Well, you can see how lovely it is."

She told me, "Today we will have a good swim."

And I said, "Of course."

When I finished eating I took the dishes back to the kitchen and asked Señora Lola if there was something I could help her with.

"I think we have everything ready. Now if you would like to go for a swim, go ahead. When the people start to come, we will be busy."

I went to my room to change. María saw me and said, "Wait for me. I'm going swimming, too."

"I am waiting for you."

She came out. I always liked to see María in her bathing suit, she was attractive, and her skin was so pretty it made me want to touch her. I was afraid to get too close to her. I might do something; then I would lose my job.

"Bueno, I am ready now. Let's go."

We started running to the water, and I couldn't help touching her somehow. Near the water I caught her by the shoulders and threw her in. "Don't do that!" she said.

"Oh, María, this is only water. You don't have to be afraid of water." She got close to me and pushed me, too, into the water. I stood up and told her, "I hope you are happy now." I caught her hand and pulled her into the water.

"Bueno," I said, "You're not going to push me into the water any more."

"No, no, I wouldn't," she said.

We dove under the water and started swimming.

"María, are you going out to the plancha today? The tide is out and it's far away."

"I don't know."

"Don't you think you could try?"

"Well, all right. If anything happens to me, you'll be responsible."

"Oh, come on, you're a good swimmer."

We started swimming all the way to the plancha. By the time we got there, we both were so exhausted we lay up there and relaxed for a while.

Finally María said, "I've had enough. I'm getting cold. Let's go back to the sand, where it's warm."

"Bueno. Let's go." We dove off into the water and started swimming out. We got to shore and lay in the sand. I lay on my back and María was lying on her stomach. She put her hand in mine. I looked at her and laughed. I said to myself, I think this girl wants to do something with me. María was smiling and laughing. Pretty soon Omar came.

Omar said to María, "Buenos días, María."

María said buenos días to him. "I see you've come late today."

He told her, "Sometimes at the jail we get off early; sometimes we get off late. Come on, let's go for a swim."

She told him, "No, I just finished swimming. If you want to swim, the ocean is right there."

I knew that Omar liked María very much, but María didn't care about him at all. She didn't even want to talk to him.

"Bueno, I'm going to swim alone. I can see this morning you are holding hands with your employee."

"Yes, we are holding hands. I like him and it is not your business what we do together." When she told him that, I put my arm around her—just what I had been waiting for. Omar looked at me jealously and meanly. He walked down to the water to swim by himself and María and I watched him.

I picked up María's hand. "Come on, let's go." We walked, holding hands, to the café and María's father saw us. He looked at me.

Her father called her, "María, come here."

She went to him. "Here I am, father."

He asked her, "Why is Layachi holding your hand?"

"I held his hand first. Then he held my hand. There is nothing wrong with that."

"Bueno, María. I hope you know what you are doing."

"Father, you don't have to worry about me. I am nineteen now. I know what I am doing."

"All right. I hope so."

"Please, father, don't think about it any more."

Señor José said to me, "Layachi, you go ahead and take a shower and get dressed. Get the keys to the dressing rooms."

"All right, Señor José."

I showered and I got the keys and sat outside waiting on the terrace. When anyone came I gave him the key and showed him which room. In a little while Omar came. He went inside and asked Señor José for a beer. He said, "Do you know what I saw today?"

"No."

"Layachi was embracing your daughter."

Señor José said, "Well, what do you think we should do now?"

"Your employee was hugging your daughter, and now you're asking me what I think we should do?"

"If my daughter likes him, there is nothing I can do about it. If my daughter likes him, it's their business, not mine. If she didn't like him and he touched her, it would be a different thing."

"Why doesn't your daughter like me? Look how long I've been coming here," Omar said. "She doesn't like me. No, she likes that poor man. He's no good. Why don't you talk to María? I am a guard at the jail. If she liked me, it would be much better for her. I work for the government. I have a good job. I make good money. I'm not like him. He is only your employee. How much money is he making here a day?"

"He earns three rials a day and his food. The money he makes is enough for him. He doesn't spend his money foolishly."

"What are you saying to me? You mean if he decides to marry your daughter, three rials a day is enough to support her?"

"If he likes my daughter and she likes him, they are going to get married. It would not be difficult for them to earn enough money. My daughter is educated and she could get a good job. I see he is a good person and my daughter likes him. I do not interfere in her life. You know my daughter is an educated girl. If I let her go, she would be working tomorrow in the best place in Tangier."

"Oh, yes, I can see that she would work in the best place. But the women should not support the men."

"That is not the way it is. People who like each other should be together and take care of each other. If two people really love each other, anything in the world they really want they will be able to get. Otherwise, if the people are not sincere, it would be different. They would be strained."

Omar said, "I would really like to know why your daughter doesn't like me. I invite her to the cinema and she never says we should go."

"Now, what do you think I should do in order to make my daughter like you?"

"All right, all right, that's enough. I'm sorry you don't want to hear the truth about Layachi."

"Why don't you look at the truth yourself? If María likes him and not you, how can I change it?"

"Really I don't know. Give me another beer." José gave him another beer. He paid and left.

María said, "Tomorrow is Saturday. The next day is Sunday. Are you still thinking that we will go to the cinema?"

"Sure, if you haven't changed your mind."

"I haven't. I would like to go."

"Now, how are we going to do it? I sleep here at night and watch the place. If we go to the cinema from ten to twelve, something might happen."

"No, it's the summer. No one will bother now."

"Bueno."

"I will ask my father. I'll see what he says."

"Bueno."

It was getting late and people started to leave.

Señor José called me: "Layachi, come here. Today we worked hard and we are tired. We are leaving now. You know how to finish up."

"Yes, Señor José."

They gathered their things together.

Señora Lola said, "Layachi, your food is in the kitchen. You know where everything is."

"Bueno, Señora Lola, muchas gracias."

María said, "Buenas noches, Layachi."

"Buenas noches, María."

"I hope you have pleasant dreams tonight."

"I hope I have some nice dreams and see someone like you."

She laughed, and they left. I cleaned the ashtrays. I finished all my work. I went to the refrigerator to get a Coca-Cola and went to the terrace.

People were leaving, and only a few were left. The moon started coming up. The moon was full and very beautiful. The most beautiful things I saw on the beach were in the evening and early morning. I liked this place, especially the job. I stayed there until it began to get late.

I am tired, I thought. If Allah wills, I will wake up early and start my work tomorrow. I went to my bed, took my clothes off, and slept till the next morning. When I awoke I went about my work as usual. I prepared the café, and soon they came in.

"Buenos días, Layachi."

"Buenos días," I said.

"Did you sleep well?"

"Yes, did you?"

María asked, "What did you dream last night?"

"I dreamed something. I don't remember what it was."

"I dreamed, too, When I woke up I thought you were there in bed with me."

"If you think you dreamed I was with you, then some day I really will be."

They started making food for the day and Señora Lola made café con leche. I took bread and butter and started to eat breakfast. María fried two eggs and poured a café con leche, and she said, "Today is a beautiful day. Look how lovely it is. I will always remember how beautiful the beach is."

"Do you think there is a better beach than this one?"

"I don't know."

We talked as we were eating. I took the dishes back to the kitchen. I asked Señora Lola if she had something for me to do. She told me I could clean the fish. I said, Bueno. I cleaned them all and put them on a plate.

"Bueno. The fish is ready and only needs to be fried."

Señora Lola said, "Put them in the refrigerator."

"Is there anything else for me to do?"

"No, not right now."

"Bueno, Señora Lola. María, are you going swimming today?"

She said, "No, today I am only going to lie on the sand. Let's go down to the water. You can go in swimming and I'll lie on the sand. Wait while I put my swim suit on."

She changed into her swim suit. She had the figure of a woman and not a young girl. We ran all the way down to the water.

"Layachi, you go ahead. I'll be waiting here on the sand."

"Bueno." I jumped into the water. After, I came out of the water and went to María. My hair was wet and I shook it over her.

"Layachi, that water is cold."

"That's what you think."

I was lying close to her. I asked her, "We are talking today and tomorrow, today and tomorrow. Sometimes we play games; we touch each other. What do you think of me? Do you like me?"

"Yes, Layachi, I like you very much."

"María, I think we both like each other. What will happen if we fall in love with one another? Perhaps something will happen between us."

In a few minutes María's mother called me: "Layachi, Layachi, come here. Take a shower and get dressed because the people are coming. And María, get dressed, too."

I went and dressed and started taking people to the rooms. Lots of people came. The place was busy and the work was nice. We were busy all day long, till about five in the afternoon.

Señora Lola said, "You must be hungry. Won't you have something to eat now?"

"Yes, I would like to eat."

"What would you like? There's fried fish and shrimp and paella."

"Yes, I would like paella."

She filled a plate and gave it to me. I took a fork and asked, "Señor José, may I have a Coca-Cola?"

"Layachi, you do not have to ask me. Next time you go to the frigidaire and take it yourself."

"Muchas gracias." I opened the Coca-Cola and went to the

terrace and ate till I was full and said thanks to Allah for today. I took the dishes back to the kitchen. I went back out to the terrace. In a few minutes María filled a plate with paella and brought a beer and came to sit with me.

"Layachi, do you drink beer?"

"No."

"Wine?"

"No."

She finished eating and took the empty bottle and glass back to the kitchen.

I went to the kitchen and I told Señora Lola, "You have been working, so let us wash the dishes and you sit down."

"Yes, Layachi, muchas gracias."

María said, "Mama, you work very hard, so you relax. Go and sit."

Señora Lola said, "Yes, yes." Señora Lola made café con leche and she went to her husband and they began to talk together.

María and I were washing the dishes and we talked and laughed until we finished the work. María said, "Now let's go out and sit in the sun for a while." We sat out on the terrace.

I said to María, "Tomorrow is Sunday. Did you talk to your father? Are we going to the cinema?"

"No I didn't. Now is a good time for me to talk to him. Wait here, I will go inside and ask him."

María went inside and she was talking with her mother and father. They were laughing. They talked for a while.

María came back. "Layachi, it's all set. Tomorrow we are going to the cinema."

"What time will we go?"

"Tomorrow we work late, until about eight o'clock. The cinema starts at ten. We'll go home and relax. You finish your work; then you come to my house and we will go from there."

"Bueno."

"Today my father will pay you."

"I wouldn't mind if your father paid me right now. I need shoes. I will have time to go buy them."

"Bueno. You wait here. I'm going to tell him." She went inside.

Señor José said, "Layachi, come. You need your money?"

"Yes."

He opened the drawer and gave me the money.

"I need some time to go and buy the shoes."

"Bueno, go ahead."

I walked to the only bacal nearby. You could buy all the different things that you needed there. I walked to the man in the bacal and asked him for shoes.

I said, "Let me try a pair and see if they fit."

"Let me see your foot."

He looked at my feet and gave me a pair. I tried them. "These are too tight. I would like to try a larger size."

He gave me a larger pair and I put those on. I liked the way they fit. I said, "How much?"

He said, "Ten rials." I paid him and walked back to the beach carrying the new shoes. I had a little money left. I said to myself, I will save this money and then buy some new clothes when I can. I went back to the café.

Señor José asked, "Did you buy the shoes?"

"Yes."

"Let's see them. Oh, these will look good on you."

"Muchas gracias, Señor José."

"Bueno, now we are going to leave. You finish up your work."

Señora Lola said, "Layachi, there is food in the kitchen fixed for you."

"Bueno. Muchas gracias, Señora Lola."

They gathered up their things and said, Buenas noches. Señor José and Señora Lola went out. María went into the kitchen and called me. "Layachi, come here. I want to show you something.

I'll show you a little work for you to do. Get close. You can see these things here?"

"What things? Where?"

"This faucet here. It needs to be fixed."

"What for? What faucet? What's wrong with it?"

I looked over the sink and she put her head close to me in order to look, too. I kissed her. When I kissed her, she hugged me tightly and kissed me very, very hard. We began to feel much closer toward each other.

Her mother called her, "María, come on. Let's go."

They left. I did my work. Like every day. I said to myself, I will make café con leche. I made café con leche and sat out on the terrace looking at the ocean, waiting for the sun to set. I didn't know what lay beyond. If it is Allah's will, perhaps some day I will go to another country, I thought. I would like to see parts of the world.

It was getting dark. I went inside to turn the light on. I will eat something, I thought. I went to the kitchen, but there was so much food I couldn't choose what to eat. I went to bed.

In the morning I got up. I fixed everything the same as always, while it was still cool. In an hour or so they came in.

"Buenos días, Layachi."

"Buenos días, Señor José and Señora Lola."

Señora Lola made breakfast. People began to arrive. It was Sunday. I showed people to the dressing rooms all day. Sundays were always busy. Early in the afternoon, I started to get hungry. I saw the café was full. I went to Señora Lola and said, "I am hungry. Do you have something to give me? There are so many people right now, if you make me a bocadillo, that would be fine."

She put two eggs together on bread and I started eating. I finished the bocadillo. There were lots of people and all the dressing rooms were in use. More people came to ask for rooms. I had to tell them, "I am sorry, they are all full. There are no more." Sometimes when I took the people to give them the keys, they gave me a tip, maybe a peseta or two. That day I made good tips. That was a good day and I liked it very much. We were working all day long. There were sitll lots of people when María came out and said, "Layachi, come on. I'll show you the house where we live. When you finish your work you come there. We'll go to the cinema. Do you see this big street? Its name is Avenida de España. See that white house up there where I point with my finger? We live there in the second floor, number four. As soon as all the people are gone, finish your work, then come up to the house."

"Bueno," I said, "I will be there."

"You see how busy it is. I am going inside to help."

Finally people started leaving. At eight-thirty in the evening there were still three men left in the café.

Señor José called me and said, "If you want to pick up the chairs on the terrace, you can do it. No one is sitting out there now."

"Bueno," I said. I put the chairs close to the door and the three men left.

"Layachi."

"Yes, Señor."

"Now you go ahead and finish up your work, then come to the house. I know you and María are going to the cinema tonight. We are leaving now. We are very tired."

"Yes, Señor."

And they left. I cleaned the ashtrays and finished all the work. I went to the kitchen and there was food that Señora Lola had left. I ate. I lit a cigarette. I didn't know what time it was. I said to myself, I should go now. I closed all the doors and windows and put the keys in my pocket. I walked to the house. I knocked on the door. Señora Lola opened the door. "Layachi, come in." I went inside and sat down. Señora Lola asked me if I wanted something to drink.

"Wine or beer, or whatever you like."

"If you have some coffee, that would be good."

She fixed a glass of coffee for me.

"Señora Lola, what time is it?"

"It is near nine-thirty."

"Bueno. Where is María?"

"She is in her room getting dressed."

In a few minutes María came out, wearing a dress I had never seen her in before, and she had on an attractive perfume. She was so lovely standing there and I had the feeling I would like to kiss her.

"Layachi, are you ready?"

"No, let me finish my coffee first. María, you look prettier than I've ever seen you look before." She sat down next to me on the couch.

They had a fancy house with nice furnishings. That was the first time I had been in María's house. These people were good and I liked them very much. When I finished my coffee, I said, "María, are you ready to go now?"

"Yes, bueno, I've been ready for a long time."

"Let's go. Buenas noches, Señora Lola."

We walked to the cinema. When we got there, I went to the ticket window to get two tickets, one for her and one for me.

María said, "No, Layachi, you buy yours and I'll buy mine."

"María, I am the man and I should get your ticket, too."

"No, you don't have enough money. You pay your way and I'll pay mine."

"Bueno, it's all right." She gave me a rial, and I had a rial. I bought the tickets and we went inside. The cinema hadn't started yet. We were looking for seats and people were staring at us. María was dressed up. My clothes weren't so good. There were a lot of people.

—Look, look, a poor man with a Spanish girl.

—That poor man with that beautiful Spanish girl.

—See how pretty she is.

—He isn't good enough for her.

They whispered and I could feel what they were thinking.

We sat down. There were three young men sitting behind us. They were saying that I wasn't good enough to be with this girl. I began to get confused with people saying all these things.

"He isn't worth her," one of them said. An old woman heard this and said to the young man, "You see that he respects her, and if they both like each other, no one can come between them. Look. She likes him and he likes her. Why do you want to gossip about other people? You don't have anything better to do than talk about others and gossip?"

The young man got very quiet. María and I changed our seats. María said, "It's very warm."

"If you want to take off your sweater, go ahead."

She took off her sweater and her hair fell over her shoulders. It seemed everyone was watching her, looking at her with me. I had on old clothes. The only good thing I had was my new shoes. After María took off her sweater, she conspicuously put her arm around my shoulder. Everyone could see. We started talking.

"María, what do you think, with these people talking like this?"

"I'm not interested in what anyone else has to say."

"Yes, people should all be like you, María."

The lights went out and the cinema started. María moved closer to me. In a little while I smelled kif. The young men sitting in back of us were smoking.

"Layachi, I'm getting very dizzy with this smell."

"If you are getting dizzy, why don't you come sit here with us, and we'll stop smoking," one of the three men said to her. "You are sitting there with him. What for? All he has is a new pair of shoes. What do you like in him?"

María was quiet. She didn't say anything. Another one said, "Ay, ay, ay, you think you brought some kind of official with you. He doesn't even know how to walk in the street, and you brought him with you to the cinema to make us feel ashamed. Shame on you."

The three of them were talking. "Do you know I have one pipe of kif? It is better than him."

She said nothing. In a few minutes Jalali came, a police inspector who had a Spanish girlfriend. She was beautiful. I saw them and said, "Ah, Jalali."

He said, "Who is that?"

"Layachi."

"Oh, yes."

"There are seats here. Come on, sit down here."

"Are there two seats?"

"Yes."

He was holding his girlfriend's hand. They sat down in the same row near us.

"Jalali, do you know this girl? She is my friend."

"No, what is her name?"

"María."

"Do you know my friend? Her name is Nina."

Nina said to me, "Did the cinema just start?"

"Yes, only five or ten minutes ago. How are you, Nina?"

"Fine. And how are you, Layachi?"

"Fine."

Jalali and I were talking.

One of the young men said, "Well, well, I see another official has come in."

Jalali asked, "Layachi, did you hear what he said?"

"Yes, we've been sitting here. And they've been making jokes about us, the three of them."

"I think I smell kif."

"Yes, they are smoking kif."

"Wait a minute. Nina, will you change seats with me so that I can sit closer to them?" Nina was sitting next to María. They changed seats. Pretty soon Jalali got up.

"I'll be right back."

I asked, "Are you going to buy something?"

"Yes," and he went out. He was gone for a few minutes and came back.

"What happened? What did you buy?"

"Oh, nothing. Just listen now. We will watch two movies now—one in the front, one in the back." We laughed. We were watching the cinema and the three in back were smoking. Pretty soon a policeman came in.

"Okay, let's go," the policeman said. And he took the three. We didn't know what they were talking about outside. The policeman came back in and said, "Jalali, they have a jar of kif and a pipe. What do you think? Can I take them to the police station until the morning?"

"No, don't do that. Just take the kif away from them and let them go." The policeman went out. We didn't see him any more.

"Layachi, what do you think?"

"They were giving us a headache. I am glad they are gone."

María said, "I am going to watch this cinema now."

"Bueno, María, go ahead. The problem is over now." María put her head on my shoulder and relaxed to watch the cinema. It was over at twelve o'clock and we left.

"María, now I will take you home, then go on down to the café."

"Bueno."

We walked to her house. I hugged her and kissed her. "I don't know where this relationship is going to get us. We went to the cinema: now, everyone is talking about us and saying different things."

"I am not interested in other people or in what they say."

"Yes, María, thank you. I appreciate that. People should love each other this way. Buenas noches, María."

"Buenas noches."

I walked down to the beach. I got to the café and lit the light. I made the bed and went to sleep until morning. I woke up and washed my face.

I took the tables and chairs out. I took the ashtrays and put one on every table. Everything was set up nicely. When I finished the work, I sat on one of the chairs. Soon María, Señor José and Señora Lola came in.

"Buenos días," they said.

"Buenos días," I said.

María's father had two big baskets of food. They started to prepare the food like every other day. That morning María made coffee. María gave me a glass of café con leche.

"Layachi, what did you think of that cinema last night?"

"The cinema was very nice, but some of the people wouldn't let us enjoy it."

"Layachi, stop thinking about those people; let them say whatever they like, it doesn't matter."

"Yes, you're right."

We finished breakfast and I asked, "Señora Lola, do you have anything for me to do?"

"No, not now."

I went out to ask María if she wanted to go swimming.

She said, "Not now. It's still too cold." I told her it was nice in the early morning.

"Bueno, if you want me to go with you, wait until I get my swimsuit on."

María went to the dressing room to put on her suit. I waited on the terrace for her. We ran to the water and jumped in quickly.

"Layachi, the water is cold."

We swam for a little bit.

María said, "I'm going out. It's too cold."

"Bueno, go ahead." María went to lie on the sand and I continued swimming until I had enough. I went close to María and lay next to her. I turned around and saw Omar coming.

"María, it looks like Omar is coming early this morning."

"Oh, yes, sometimes he comes early."

He walked toward us.

"Buenos días, María."

"Buenos días, Omar. How are you this morning?"

"As you can see, here I am. You are looking very beautiful this morning."

"Thank you."

"Did you go to the cinema?"

"Yes, we went last night, Layachi and I. But we found bad people up there who couldn't keep quiet. They always find something to talk about."

"Do you remember I told you, as long as you keep going with a poor man, nobody will like what you do."

"Bueno, bueno, please stop talking now, Omar. It's very early in the morning and you give me a headache. If you want to go swimming, go ahead; the ocean is right there."

"María, every time I try to talk to you, you get mad."

"If we are only talking, why don't you talk about something else and leave my friends alone? I told you that this man knows Spanish, so if you say something, he understands."

"Bueno, María, I know you get mad quick. But tell me, will you go with me to the cinema next Sunday? I am inviting you before Sunday comes."

María said, "I told you. I'm not going anywhere with you. I'm sure you can find someone else to take to the movies. Layachi, come on, let's go to the café."

Chapter Four

The Stolen Wallet

We walked back to the café. I went into the shower, put on my clothes and sat down on the terrace. María dressed, came out and sat beside me. We were talking. Monday mornings there were always slow.

An hour later María said, "I think I'll go inside to help in the kitchen. People are arriving now."

"Bueno." And people started asking for dressing rooms. An English lady came in then, changed her clothes, and lay down on the beach. A few minutes later she stood up and started shouting. "Someone's stolen my wallet!" the woman cried.

People gathered around her, to find out what had happened. One man said, "Was anyone else near you?"

"No," she said.

"What about that man up there?" he asked. When he pointed at me, the crowd turned and saw me on the terrace.

Omar showed up soon after this. "What's happening here? What's going on?"

"That English woman—somebody stole her wallet."

"Who?"

"That one up there," the man replied. Then he pointed his hand at me.

"Leave him there," Omar said. "We're going to call the police." There were always one or two policemen patrolling on the beach where people swam. A man from the crowd found one and brought him back. I heard them tell him, "Someone stole this English woman's wallet. One of us saw who did it. He's there, at the café."

The policeman came to Omar. I was watching. Omar pointed at me. "That one! He's the one who stole the wallet."

The policeman came to me. "Okay, let's go."

"Where? Where are we going? What for?"

"The English woman says you stole her wallet. We're going to the commissariat."

"She says I stole her wallet? She saw me?"

He called the woman over. He asked her if she saw me steal the wallet.

"No, I didn't see him," the woman said. "I didn't see anybody near me. I only know, I was lying on the beach. My wallet was right here in my bag. I turned around, to get something to drink from the bag, and then I saw that my wallet wasn't in it. I didn't see this man take anything. But this other one here says he saw him take it."

The policeman asked Omar, "Did you see him take this woman's wallet?"

"Yes, I did."

"What do you do for a living?"

"I'm a guard at the jail."

"Okay."

I had the keys to the dressing rooms. I said, "Excuse me a minute. I have to give these keys back to my boss."

I went inside the café and gave the keys to Señor José. He had been watching everything.

"Here are the keys," I said. "I think I'm going to the commissariat. Omar claims he saw me steal a woman's wallet."

Señor José came out. He said to the policeman, "This man

works for me. He keeps the keys for the dressing rooms, and gives them to the people when they change. I don't think he would steal anything from anyone. Omar, what do you have against Layachi? Is it true? Did you see him steal the wallet?"

"Now, you think I'm lying," Omar said. "Do you think I would ever lie to you?"

"I don't know what's going on around here! I've left money and my things here many times. Layachi is here all day and night. He's never taken one peseta."

Omar said, "I saw the woman lying on the beach. Then I saw Layachi go and take her wallet and hide it. I watched everything from the café."

I said, "Here I am. Why don't you search me? Search my room too. See if you can find a wallet."

The officer said, "We've already talked too much. We're wasting time." And he handcuffed me.

"Okay, let's go." And Omar and the woman came along. We started walking to the commissariat. It was a long way down into the port. Finally, we arrived and went inside.

The inspector there asked me what was wrong.

"Nothing," I said. "I don't know. An English woman says I stole her wallet."

He looked at the woman. "Did he steal from you?"

The woman only spoke a little Spanish. "I didn't see him do it," she said. "This guard says he saw him."

The inspector asked Omar for his name.

"What kind of work do you do?"

"I'm a guard at the jail."

"And is it true? Did you see the man steal a wallet?"

"Of course it's true. Do you think I'm lying? This English woman isn't going to give me anything. This man isn't going to give me anything. I'm only saying what I saw."

"Do you hear what these people are saying?" the inspector asked me.

"Yes. I hear that they're lying."

"Do you know what I'm going to tell you now?"

"No."

"I think you'd better show us where you hid the wallet. What did you do with it? You better tell us now, before it's too late. You know what a police station has for you, if you don't tell us."

"I didn't see any wallet. If I'd seen her wallet, I would have given it back to her already, so I wouldn't have to walk to the police station."

The inspector slapped me with his hand. Then he called a policeman. "Put him inside. Lock him up!"

They locked me in a separate room, alone. I don't know how long I stayed there. Maybe two or three hours later, they opened the door and asked me to come out. A policeman took me to see a different inspector. The man said, "Now: are you going to tell us where you hid the wallet?"

"Please," I said. "I've never seen the wallet. The man who says he saw me take it—there's a problem between us. I work at the café on the beach. The man who owns it has a pretty daughter. She likes me and I like her. She doesn't like Omar, this guard. That's why he's telling you lies about me. He likes her, too. Anyway, I didn't see any wallet."

The inspector said, "I'm only asking you about this wallet and what you did with it. I'm not asking you about your problems. Omar swears he saw you steal it and hide it."

"If he saw me take it and hide it, he should show you where it is. That's the only way to prove I stole it."

"I said I want *you* to tell me where it is. Then we can look for it. And let you go."

I said, "I'm sorry. I didn't see a wallet. I keep telling you. If I saw it, I would have returned it to the owner."

"I think you have a very, very hard head," the inspector said.

"My head's not hard. I'm telling you the truth. I didn't see it."

"You don't like to tell the truth then, is that it?"

"I only speak the truth. If you want me to start lying, I can do that."

"You're lying now," he said. "I want you to tell me where the wallet is. Then we can let you go."

"I didn't see a wallet."

He slapped me. "Put him inside!" he said.

A policeman took me by the hands and locked me in the room. He turned the key, then opened a little slit in the door like a window. "Everything would be easier," he said, "if you showed us where you have the wallet."

I told the man, "I haven't seen a wallet. You know what the people say?" I asked.

"What?"

"'I hope no lie falls on you,'" I said.

"You're in for a lot of trouble. And it's going to be your fault."

"What happens to me," I said, "is Allah's will."

He closed the window and left. By now, it was getting very dark. I still had no idea what time it was.

Later, they took me out again, to a room with three policemen and an inspector.

The inspector said, "Now: what do you think? Are you going to tell the truth this time, or not?"

"The truth? I already told you. I didn't see any wallet."

"Come here," he said. "Come closer."

I walked a little closer to the inspector.

He said, "It's better for you to tell the truth. Otherwise, you'll be sorry. But feeling sorry isn't going to help you. Not with us."

I said, "I've told you, I saw no wallet. I guess there's nothing more for me to say."

One of the policemen slapped my face. I put my hand to my face, then turned around, and another man slapped me. I was caught there between the three policemen. They slapped me and hit me, tossing me around from one to the other. I said nothing. Wherever I turned, a hard hand hit my body.

At last I said, "I told you I didn't see a wallet, because I didn't. Do you want me to lie? I don't know how."

Then they began to hit me with their fists and kick me, too. I lost all patience.

"What *is* this?"

The inspecdtor said, "Be quiet. You stole the wallet and you hid it. Now, you're going to tell us where it is. A man who works as a guard in the jails wouldn't lie about a thing like this."

"But I told you why Omar is lying! Believe what I tell you, or don't. It's up to you."

"Who's going to believe you? You're lying!"

"I know you don't believe me. I can see that. If you believed me, you would have let me go. Instead, you're beating me to death. You're all corrupt!"

Before I could finish, an officer hit me in the face.

"You're still not going to tell the truth?"

I said, "I told you."

"Okay. Give him some more," the inspector said.

They kept it up, beating me, then asking me, until they saw that I was almost unconscious. They kept talking to me. I couldn't speak. The inspector stood up then. He slapped me twice.

"Take him inside," he said.

They opened the door again and threw me in.

I lay there on the floor all night, talking to myself. I was still a kid. Okay, Allah, I said, you see what's happening. You know what they do to honest people. Is that why I'm supposed to take all this? If this is how it's supposed to be, all right.

I stayed there all night shivering, by myself. In the morning they brought hot tea and a loaf of bread. I drank the tea, and left the bread alone. Finally, they opened up the door.

I went out and met a new inspector.

"Tell the truth and I'll let you go, right now."

I said, "They were beating me to death last night. Look at my face. You can see for yourself. If I had something else to say, I would have said."

"Larbi," he said, "what's wrong with you?"

"Can't you see?" I said. My face was swollen.

"So, you don't want to tell the truth."

"I have already."

"Sit down," he said.

I sat down on a chair opposite the desk.

"What's your name?" he asked me.

"Larbi."

"Larbi, what?"

"Larbi Layachi."

"Where do you live?"

"In Monopolio. Near the tobacco factory."

"Are you married?"

"No."

"What's your mother's name?"

I said, "Fatima."

"Father's name?"

"My father's name is Larbi."

The inspector took all this down on a typewriter.

"And you're still not going to tell the truth for us?"

"I have," I said.

He went on typing words I couldn't see, filled out his report, and gave it to me. "Here, sign it."

"Why should I sign it?"

"You have to sign it. This is a report."

"I don't know what's on it," I said.

"Everything you were talking about," he said.

"I wasn't talking about anything. What is it I'm saying?"

"If you want me to read it to you, I can," he said.

"If you want to read it, fine. If you don't, I won't sign."

"If you don't, we'll keep you here three or four more days. And what happened to you last night, will happen again. Maybe something worse. It says here that we have a witness, who saw you steal the English woman's wallet."

"All those pages, and that's all it says?"

He stood up and slapped me. "What are you going to do?"

I said to myself, Allah, I don't think that I can fight this fire.

"Okay, I'll sign."

Since I couldn't write, they pressed my thumb on a pad of ink and rolled the print it made across each page. Then they hand-cuffed me. A Jeep came and took me to the courthouse.

I found a judge and jury sitting there. My name was called.

"Larbi Layachi?"

"Yes."

"Come closer."

I walked closer.

"Sit down."

I sat.

"We have a report here. It says you stole a wallet from an English woman."

"Sir," I said, "I didn't steal from her. I work at a café on the beach. The day this happened, I was waiting there with the keys in my hand for the people who come to rent the dressing rooms. That's what I do at the café. I was on the terrace. If this woman saw with her own eyes, maybe it would be a different story. But the only one who claims I stole from her, is a guard named

Omar. Omar and I don't get along. We have a problem at the place where I work. There is a girl there, the boss's daughter. Once in a while we swim together; sometimes we go to the cinema. We like each other. When Omar comes to see her, she doesn't want to talk to him. That's the problem. That's why he's lying."

The judge said, "Your problems are not my business. What I'm looking at is this report. If you tell the truth right now, I'll let you go."

I said, "I didn't see a wallet. I didn't steal a wallet."

The judge wrote something down on a piece of paper, then he handed the paper to a policeman. The policeman put handcuffs on my wrists, and said, "Let's go." They put me into a van with some other men and took us to the jail in the Casbah.

A guard stood at the door inside the jail. The policeman gave my papers to the guard, and then they searched us one by one. I was with six others. They searched me and didn't find anything. From there they put us into a crowded cell. My friend Mimun, the trusty, was in there with them.

"Larbi," he said, "hello. You're back again? What have you done? What is it, this time?"

I said, "This time it's very bad. It's worse."

"What did you do?"

"Omar says he saw me steal a wallet. I'm working at the beach. There's a girl there, who likes me. Omar likes her too. He's told some lies about me, because he's jealous."

"A prison guard says he saw you? That's a complicated story."

"Yes, because of the girl at the beach. I'm working for her father. The girl is beautiful. But Omar thinks he's better than me, because he works for the government and makes more money. People who work for the government can do anything they please. He can't see why she's going out with me. He wants her."

"Very complicated," Mimun said. "I don't know what to tell you. Sometimes your mind and soul are put to the test. All you can do is endure it. Are you hungry?"

"A little."

Mimun took me to his room. Because he was the *muqaddim* he had a separate place here. He gave me a little beef stew and some bread.

"Don't worry about it," he told me. "If that's the way it's going to be, that's how it's going to happen."

"It's all right," I said. "It doesn't matter."

I finished eating and asked him for a cigarette. "I didn't bring any with me. I need one badly."

He opened a carton and handed me a pack. "Come on," he said. "I'll show you where you're going to sleep."

He took me into a room that was like a tunnel, full of prisoners. He found a place for me and gave me a mat. I set the mat on the floor, then spread two blankets on the top.

He said, "If you need more blankets, I'll try to find them."

"Thanks," I said. "This will be enough."

When other prisoners asked me what I'd done to be put in jail, I said, "It doesn't matter. I've already told the story a hundred times."

Some of the men were playing cards. Others were playing dominoes, doing something to help the time go by. I went over to a group that was playing cards and sat and watched. Then a guard knocked on the door. He said, *It's time to count!*

Mimun told everyone, "Okay, let's go. Everyone stand in two lines, one in front of the other." We had to stand this way, because the guards always counted us by twos. When they finished counting, they closed the door and left. Then everybody went back to their places.

One man said, "I'm tired of playing cards. Larbi, do you

want to play my hand?"

"Sure."

We stayed there playing, talking and smoking cigarettes. Then a guard knocked on the door again. The guard said, *Soup!* They brought it in and Mimun divided up the soup between us. Everyone had his bowl. It wasn't good, but those without any family to bring them food were forced to eat it. If they didn't there was nothing else to eat.

When I got the soup, I took it and sat down in my place. I looked at the soup. I wasn't hungry, because Mimun already had given me something to eat. There was a prisoner sitting near me. I asked him if he would like more soup.

"Yes," the man said. He took the soup.

I lay down on my mat and started thinking. I found a good job, I thought, and now I'll lose it, because of what Omar did to me. I hope some day Allah will punish him. Only the poor people suffer in this world. I wonder why. Allah is watching everybody, it's true. But where are you going to find the truth? And where are you going to find the law? These people who make up the law only make laws that will be good for them.

In a while they knocked on the door again: *Okay, it's counting time.*

They came in to count. They finished and went out and closed the door. Mimun went with a group that was smoking kif. He called me: "Larbi, come here. What are you thinking about? What's wrong?"

I said, "It's hard, you know, when someone who hasn't done a thing has to come here and go through so much trouble."

He said, "You're just making it harder for yourself. Allah set it up this way. You have to go through it, the way it's been set up. Allah knows what's best for everyone."

He went on talking for a while, until the guards knocked twice on the door. My friend Mimun said, "Everyone go to your place now. The light is going off." Everybody went back to their places. Mimun went to his room; then they turned the light off.

Mimun called out, "Everyone go to sleep. No more talking."

At six the next morning the guards knocked on the door. We rolled up our straw mats, folded and put our blankets on the top, and began getting ready. We washed and then began to walk around. At seven they brought in tea and half a loaf of bread for each prisoner. We got in line, took our tea and bread and went to our places. At eight o'clock they knocked again and said it was counting time.

Mimun said, "Everybody get in line."

We got in line. They opened the door, came inside and counted. When they finished, I saw Omar standing there. I looked at him. He looked at me. We both knew what had happened. He still looked unhappy, even though I was locked up behind bars.

When they closed the door, I went back to my place and sat and thought. I said, Allah, it looks bad. What can I do to get out of this safely?

That night the prisoners got together and played games. I stayed in my place. I didn't feel like playing games that evening. I lay there, watching all the prisoners. Some played cards. Some only walked around in circles.

I stayed for eight days inside the jail. I was sleeping in my place about three a.m., when three guards came in and woke me up. There was Omar and two men I didn't know. They said, "Stand up!"

I was still asleep. I fell down, then they kicked me. They searched my place and found a pipe and a paper full of kif.

"Ah," they said, "you smoke kif? Don't you know it's forbidden to have kif and a pipe in prison?"

I said, "That isn't mine. I don't smoke kif."

They took me out of the cell, to a room where the guards relaxed when they weren't on duty. They began to beat me. Omar beat me with a club.

"This is for the Spanish girl at the beach."

I said he was going to eat his heart forever. I told him the Spanish girl didn't like him. "Why put yourself through all these changes? Why try to go out with someone who doesn't like you?"

He hit me again.

I knew I had no chance against three guards. I stood up and kicked Omar in the guts, and he fell down, crying like a baby. I kicked him in the face as he was falling. Then the guards clubbed me three times and I fell. Lying face down, I heard them talking.

Omar said, "Keep hitting him!"

The others said, "That's enough. We've taught him a lesson. He'll never go out with a Spanish girl again."

They picked me up, took me to my place, and threw me in.

Mimun heard the noise and came in. He said, "My God, look what they did to him! What happened?"

I said, "I told you. Omar is jealous. He can't stop thinking about it. In the morning, I'm going to the warden."

A couple of hours later, they knocked on the door and said, *Get up!*

We got up and washed and walked around. An hour later they brought breakfast, tea and half a loaf of bread. I took the tea and bread, but I couldn't eat. My face was swollen. My body ached all over. I'd never been beaten up like this before.

I waited until nine o'clock, when Monsieur Japont, the warden, came into his office. I told Mimun, "It's time. I want to go out, now."

Mimun knocked on the door. The guard came and opened it. "What's the matter?"

Mimun said, "We have a man who was beaten up last night. He wants to see the warden."

The guard said, "Okay." he closed the door and went to the office. The warden told the guard to bring me out.

The guard came back and called, "Mimun! Mimun!"

Mimun said, "Yes?"

The guard said, "Bring the prisoner."

Mimun and the guard helped me walk across the street into the office. I went in. The warden looked at me.

"What happened?"

I said, "This morning I was sleeping. Three guards came in and woke me up. They took me out and beat me. They accused me of having kif inside my cell. Now, I want some justice."

He said, "Okay, you go back to your cell. I'll talk to the guards. I'll find out why they did it."

Mimun and the guard and I walked back to the jail.

A few days later the warden laid off Omar and his friends. He laid them off for three months, without pay. A guard was forbidden to go into a cell without the warden, and the warden was very strict and straight. He did his job. He treated everybody fairly.

When the prisoners heard what happened to Omar and the guards, they all thanked Allah. Allah, they said, was the real judge of everyone on earth. I never saw Omar there again.

I stayed in jail ten more days. One morning they called me into court. The judge announced my name and I stood up.

He said, "Did you steal this wallet?"

"No, Your Honor, I did not. I had a problem with a guard up at the jail. He was angry with me. The daughter of the man I work for didn't want to go out with him. He was mad, because she was going out with me."

The judge said, "I'm not interested in that. Just tell us: did you steal the wallet?"

"No," I said. "If you don't believe me, send for the man I work for on the beach. His name is Señor José. He owns the café there. Ask him if I ever stole from him."

The judge said, "Fine. Go downstairs. We'll call you, when we've sent for your employer."

I went downstairs and waited. They sent for Señor José and brought him back. They called me back again in half an hour. When I came in, Señor José was sitting with the public. The judge called me closer to the bench.

"Señor José," he said, "does this man work for you?"

"Yes."

"And has he ever stolen anything?"

"No, Your Honor. I leave money at the café every morning. I never found anything missing."

"That's all. Sit down."

I sat down. Señor José sat down too. Then the three judges began to talk together.

"Layachi! Stand up."

I stood up.

The judge said, "This is the second time you've been here. We don't like people coming back to jail. The English woman says she didn't see you steal her wallet. But there was a witness there who said you did."

I said, "Your Honor, if he saw me take the wallet, have him tell you where I hid it. The police searched me and they searched my room. They didn't find anything."

They called Omar in, to be a witness, but Omar wasn't in the room.

The judge said, "Layachi, we're going to give you one more chance. But we don't want you back in here again."

I said, "I swear, if I can stay out of trouble, I'll never come back here. Now, I've lost my job. God knows where I'm going to find a new one."

He said, "We going to give you three months in jail. The next time you come back, we're going to send you to prison for two years."

I went downstairs. I waited until they had sentenced all the prisoners, then the wagon came and took us back to jail. When I walked in, Mimun said, "Well, what happened?"

I said, "I got three months."

He said, "That isn't bad. You've already served five weeks of that."

I said, "I wish I'd really stolen the wallet. I wouldn't feel so bad."

He said, "You didn't steal it?"

I said, "No."

Now that I'd been sentenced, they let me go outside during the day, to work in the king's garden up the street. Eight of us went up there every morning. Sometimes tourists came to see the palace. When we begged, they gave us money to buy cigarettes and bread. Sometimes we even went to a café, which wasn't far, and ordered tea. I stayed in prison, today and tomorrow, until I only had three days to serve.

One afternoon some new inmates arrived. I began to ask them why they'd been arrested. I found two men among them—one named Mohammed and one named Abdallah. They had been arrested for raping a ten-year-old.

Chapter Five

The Two Rapists

I asked the two new prisoners in the jail where they had come across the boy. They said they had found him in the medina. He was poor, they said, and had no food or money. He lived with his mother and his stepfather. This reminded me of myself at about his age, when I was living with my stepfather.

I said, "You both made love to him?"

Mohammed was a man of thirty-five. Abdallah, his lover, was younger. He was twenty. Still, Mohammed became tired of making love to him. He told Abdallah, "Go find me a boy, if you want to go on staying here and living off my money." He said, "Abdallah, you're getting old. I want to make love with someone younger."

Abdallah went out walking in the medina. There he found a hungry ten-year-old. He took the boy to a restaurant and bought a plate of food, then took him to a café and bought him tea. He asked the boy if he would like to come home with him. Then they went together to Mohammed's, outside Tangier, in a village called the Charf.

Mohammed had a wonderful house out there. He was well-to-do.

They walked up to the bus station in the Socco. When the bus came, they rode it to the Charf. They got off at the bottom of the hill, then walked up the mountain to Mohammed's. Abdallah had been given his own key. He opened the door and let the boy inside. The house was empty. Mohammed was in his orchard, picking fruit. They sat in the sala talking, until Mohammed came back in.

"Ahilan," he said.

They said, "Ahilan."

Mohammed cooked dinner and Abdallah helped him. The boy sat watching everything. When they had eaten and had their tea, Mohammed said to Abdallah, "Leave. Come back a little later."

Abdallah went out for a walk.

While he was gone, Mohammed told the boy that he wanted to make love to him. He promised him that, if he would make love, the boy could live here, instead of with his stepfather. The stepfather had never liked the boy.

The boy thought about it. Finally, he let Mohammed have his way. Mohammed made love to him, but he wasn't careful. Instead of going slowly, he tore the boy. The boy began to cry and cry.

When Abdallah returned, he opened the door and found the boy still weeping. He said, "What happened?"

"I was making love to him," Mohammed said, "but it wouldn't fit. I think he's bleeding."

"I thought you were going to be careful! You promised."

"I couldn't help myself," Mohammed said. "Look at him. How beautiful he looks! He looks like a girl, not a boy."

Of course, the boy was ten years old. How could he look.

The boy kept crying. Mohammed and Abdallah kept talking. Abdallah had brought the boy up here; Mohammed, of course, was guilty too. They decided to bribe him. They would offer the boy five thousand francs, not to tell anything to anyone, and not to say that this had happened to him at Mohammed's. Finally, the boy stopped crying. They didn't get to sleep until two o'clock. Mohammed and Abdallah slept together. The boy slept by himself on a mat.

In the morning the men got up and made breakfast. They fed the boy and gave him five thousand francs. Then they walked him to the bottom of the hill and told him to go back to his stepfather. The boy rode all the way to the Socco Kebir and got off the bus. When he got off, he saw a policeman. He ran straight to him and started crying.

The policeman said, "Aoulidi, stop crying, what's the matter? Did someone beat you?"

The boy kept crying. He didn't know what to say.

The policeman took him to the commissariat. The boy was still in tears when they walked in. An inspector and two policemen asked him what had happened. He finally told them. The boy gave the police the two men's names. He said, "They live out on the Charf."

"Can you remember where the house is?"

The boy was intelligent. He said, "Yes."

They put him into a jeep and drove up the mountain. At first, the boy seemed lost. The men kept asking questions and driving around the Charf. When they finally passed the house, the boy pointed at it with his finger. The police went to Mohammed's door and knocked. The house was empty.

"Nobody's here," said the inspector. "We'll leave. We'll come back."

They returned to the commissariat.

That afternoon they put the boy into the jeep again, and drove up to the Charf. This time when they knocked Mohammed answered. He looked at the boy and the police. He knew that the boy had already told them everything.

"Come with us," they said. And they handcuffed him.

They took him to the commissariat and beat him. Islam forbids a man to make love to boys. Of course, they all do it, but when someone gets caught it's still disgraceful.

They asked Mohammed where his friend was.

"On the street somewhere," he said.

They asked the boy, "Do you remember where he picked you up?"

The boy said, "Yes. In the medina. He took me to a café there. He bought me food and tea."

"Do you remember which café?"

The boy said, "Yes."

They put him into the jeep and drove to the medina. At the café, they asked the qaouadji, "Do you remember this boy? He was here yesterday, with a man named Abdallah."

"Yes sir," the qaouadji said. "They came in together. They had some tea and left."

They said, "Have you seen Abdallah today?"

He said, "Today? Not yet."

On their way back to the commissariat, they saw Abdallah walking down the hill to the Socco Chico. They stopped right in front of him, and handcuffed him and beat him on the street. They beat him so badly that a crowd formed. Abdallah cried out to them for help, but when the people heard what he had done, they turned away.

The police took him to the commissariat and threw him in a cell beside his friend. The two of them discussed what they would do. They knew that, if they lied, the police would beat them both to death. Already they had been beaten pretty badly. Finally, they agreed to tell the truth. The police left them alone, until three a.m. Then they unlocked the door and took them out. They were ready to start beating them again, but first they questioned them.

They said, "Did you do this to the boy?"

Both men said, "Yes."

"Everything the boy says is true?"

"Yes."

They beat them a little and put them back in jail.

At nine o'clock the next morning the inspector opened the door and brought them out. The police had finished filing their report. They asked both men to sign the papers. Mohammed and Abdallah both signed. Abdallah did the talking, but Mohammed was quiet. He was ashamed. The other prisoners in the jail couldn't even look at him.

Later, the guards knocked on the door. We lined up behind each other in double file. They came in, made their count, and left. Later, they knocked again: *Your soup is ready.* They opened the door and brought in the soup, and Mimun divided it between us. When we had eaten, the men broke up into groups and played their games. I went back and talked to the two new prisoners.

I asked them what had happened to the boy.

They didn't know. They said the policemen had him.

"What are you going to do? What do you think your punishment will be?"

They said, "Only Allah knows the truth."

I said, "How could you do a thing like this?"

Mohammed said, "Both of us didn't do it. I'm the one who raped the boy."

"How does it feel?"

He said, "It will teach me a lesson. I'll never make love to boys again."

I looked at Abdallah. I said, "Are you going to pimp anymore, for Mohammed?"

He said, "No, my friend. It's the last time."

I said, "Why do you say that? Because you're locked up behind bars, you think you'll never sin again? You're just saying that to make yourself feel good." I walked away from both of them. I went to play cards with some other men.

That day I heard a group of prisoners talking. Some said they were going to rape Abdallah, to pay him for the filthy thing he'd done, to teach him a lesson. That evening the guards knocked on the door: *The lights are going off now. Get back to your places.* We went to our places, then the lights went off.

Sometime after midnight, I woke up. I heard walking, and talking, whispering, and men going back and forth to the rapists' cell. They went to Abdallah's place and woke him up.

"Get up!"

"What's going on?"

They hit him in the face, told him to drop his pants and turn around. Then one after another they raped him. Eight or nine prisoners—Abdallah was crying all the while. Finally, Mimun woke up.

"Cut it out!" he said. "It's over."

Everybody went back to his place. We went to sleep then.

All this happened Tuesday evening.

Wednesday in the morning we all got up. We washed and walked around and then the guards knocked: *Counting-time!* they said. They came in and counted.

Abdallah looked pale. Mohammed didn't say a word. Both men stood in line without speaking. The guards finished counting and locked the door and left. The prisoners went about their business. Later, the guards knocked again: *Breakfast!* They brought our tea and bread and we ate the breakfast. Then they called the names of the men who would work at the palace. I was one of them. When the guards were ready for us, they opened up the door and said, *Let's go!*

One guard walked in front of us. Another came behind. We marched to the king's palace and worked in the garden. Because we all wore tags, the tourists who came to see the palace knew we were prisoners. Some gave us money. We worked in the garden all that afternoon. Finally, the guards said, *Let's go!* We lined up and walked back to the jail.

Inside, I went to Mimun's room.

Mimun asked me how the day had been.

I told him, "Fine."

He asked if I'd made any money, working.

I said, "Yes."

He asked how much.

I told him, "Five rials."

He asked if I needed the five rials.

I said, "Not really, why? Do you want them?"

He said, "Yes. Let me have your five rials."

I gave him the money. He had been good to me. He had given me cigarettes all the time I'd been there. I asked what he would do with the five rials. He said, "I'm going to send out for some kif. Are you hungry?"

"Yes," I said, "I'm hungry."

Mimun's family had come to visit him that day. They'd left him chicken, beef tajine and lots of bread. "Here," he said, "help yourself to what you want."

I had a wonderful meal there that evening.

When the guards knocked on the door and brought our soup, Mimun told the prisoners to get in line. They all lined up and he began to divide the soup. When he asked if I wanted soup, I told him, No. After all I had eaten, I didn't need the soup. I sat in his room until he finished.

When he returned, I said, "What happened here last night? I saw a lot of men making love to Abdallah. Did you know that was going to happen?"

Mimun said, "I heard them plan it out. But I wasn't really

interested in stopping it. Whatever happens to those two, they deserve it. The men are going to do the same thing tonight, but only to Abdallah. He's young and good looking. Mohammed looks too old to make love to."

I looked around the room. "This must be hell," I said. "If there's any hell, this is it. We're in it."

We smoked a couple of cigarettes and he made tea. Then the guards knocked on the door and said it was counting-time. They came in and counted, then closed the door and left. All the prisoners went back to their places. Those who wanted to play their games played games. I didn't want to play games, or even talk to Abdallah and Mohammed, not after what had happened here last night. I stayed in Mimun's room a while longer. Finally, the guards knocked on the door. They said, *The light will go out in five minutes. Everyone go back to your place.*

Everybody did as they were told. When the light went out, the prisoners started whispering. Loud talking now was not allowed. It got later and later, while I lay there listening in the dark. Finally, I saw shadows around Abdallah again. One by one, the men made love to him, until nobody wanted to continue. He cried all evening. It was late when I finally fell asleep.

The guards knocked on the door at six a.m. The prisoners shook their blankets and rolled up their sleeping mats. I did the same. We washed and walked around, until the guards knocked again. *It's counting-time*, they said, and they came in and counted. Then they went out and closed the door. It was my last day of watching them in the prison. The following morning, I would be released.

Mimun came to me before we ate. "What do you think?" he asked. "What are you going to do when you get out of here?"

I said, "Who knows? I guess I'll hit the streets and see what I can find."

The guards brought in our breakfast and we ate it. A while later they called through the door again for all the working prisoners to come out. We got into a line beside the door. They opened the door and we went out into the courtyard, just like every day before. We worked all day in the gardens, then they brought us back to prison. We went in and washed and relaxed for a little while, until they knocked. *Soup!* they said. And when they brought it in, Mimun divided it among us. I had some soup that evening. Then we washed our bowls, and everybody broke up into groups.

I went into Mimun's room and sat down there alone. When he came in, he said, "So, tomorrow you're going to be free."

I said, "Finally."

He said, "Be careful. Don't get yourself in trouble, or you'll come back here again."

I said, "I hope not. I never want to see this place again, if I can help it. If I can't, if I come back here again, it will just be more time wasted."

The guards came in, like every other day, made their count, then left and closed the door. We began to walk around when they were gone. A lot of the men played games again, but Abdallah and Mohammed didn't leave their places. They felt ashamed. They never had imagined, until now, that this could happen. Now they knew that you only become a sinner when you're caught. You can do what you want, as long as you want to do it, you can even molest a child if you want, and get away with it. It's when you're caught that all the shame of the world comes down on top of you. They stayed where they were and the others went on talking, until the guards knocked. *It's time,* they said, *the light is going off.* The groups broke up then. When everyone had settled in his place, the light went off and we went to sleep.

In the morning they knocked on the door at six o'clock. Everyone got up and washed as always, I went to Mimun's room. He'd already made some tea. I had a can of tea and some bread for breakfast.

"If things go well," I said, "I'll come back and see you. If they don't, I don't know what will happen."

He said, "What will you do? You have no home. You have no job. Can you go back to your mother and her husband?"

I said, "If I don't find something right away, I'll have to, for a few days, until I get something going."

He said, "Be careful. Don't get yourself in trouble. You know what's waiting for you, if you do."

They knocked on the door then. "Those who are going to be released today, get your things together."

There were seven of us. We got our things together. We didn't have much except the clothes on our backs. They opened up the door and called our names. We all stepped out. They asked us to sign a piece of paper and we signed it. Then they opened another set of doors. They said, "You're on your own. You're free." And we went out.

The men I left with asked me what I'd do.

"I don't know," I said. "I'm going to hit the streets." And we went our separate ways, through the narrow streets of the medina.

I remembered that I had left some money in my room at Señor José's, and I went down to the café to see him about it. But when I reached the place, nobody was there and it was closed. I remembered where María and her mother and father lived. I turned back and walked toward the Plaza de España, until I reached the house. I rang the doorbell.

Señora Lola answered. She said, "Layachi! You're out of jail?"

I said, "Yes. And I came to ask you if you found the money I left in my room at the café."

She said, "We found your money. Come on in."

I went inside and she handed me the money—eleven thousand francs and seven rials—exactly the amount that I had left there. She gave it to me.

Señor José was in the sala. He said, "I'm sorry for everything that happened. I still owe you money, for two days' work. Here's your money. I wish I could do more. You didn't work for us very long, but I liked you. Now, we've sold the whole café. All I can do is wish you luck."

I said, "Muchas gracias, Señor José. Now that I'm back, it's like a new life all over. Please, don't worry about your daughter. I cared for her more than you could know. But what happened between us is finished. Allah must have wanted it this way."

They said good-bye to me. They let me out.

I never saw any of them again.

Chapter Six

The Madman

The following morning I went to Souk el Kebir. I bought a kilo of apples, a kilo of pears, a kilo of bananas, and a carton of cigarettes. From the souk, I went up to the jail. I told the guard, "I've come to see my friend, Mimun, the head prisoner."

The guard said, "What's your name?"

"Layachi."

The guard went inside and called Mimun. They let me in, and brought Mimun to the visiting cell for prisoners.

I said, "Hello, Mimun. How have you been?"

"You're back. What happened?"

I said, "I picked up some back pay from the café where I used to work. I thought I'd bring you a few things you might need here."

"You don't need to do that," he said.

I said, "It's nothing compared to what I owe you."

We talked until the guard came back and said, "Your time is up." I said good-bye to Mimun and left the jail.

I walked to the Socco Chico and stopped at a café. I asked the man who ran the place if he needed any help.

"Yes," he said, "but it doesn't pay much. I can give you three rials a day, to deliver drinks to the women in the whorehouses."

This man ran three houses on the block. Each house had ten women in it. He was in charge of everything, because he was big and no one dared to challenge him.

I said, "Fine. I'll work for you."

The man served food, sodas, tea and coffee. Anytime the ladies called in an order, I took it to the house, collected the money, and brought it back to him. I became his runner. A madman, his brother, worked there too. Between themselves, they managed all the houses and the café. Each day the boss himself went out and checked the houses to be sure there were no problems and no fights.

A man named Absalem Sultane came to one of the houses every Friday. He was in love with a girl there named Aisha. He had a good job working in the port, and when he came to see her he spent a lot of money. Every time a large order came in from her house, I knew that Absalem was there.

One Tuesday after a few weeks Absalem dropped by unexpectedly, Aisha was with another client.

Absalem began to scream, "Aisha? I want to see Aisha!"

The patrona told him, "Wait. She'll be out to see you in a while. She's your girl, and you love her. We know that. We don't want to take her away from you. But we didn't know you'd be coming in tonight. She's with a date, now."

The madman's brother heard them screaming. He crossed the street and came into the house. "What's happening? What's going on here!"

Absalem Sultane stood up. "I'm in love with Aisha. I want to see her. I don't want Aisha going out with other men."

The brother said, "What do you mean? You know as well as I do, Aisha's just a whore. She's here to make money for us. You can't tell Aisha who to go with. Have you ever talked with her about it?"

"Yes, I talked with her. She loves me. I want to see her. Now! Don't I spend a lot of money here?"

"Yes. But now you're disturbing other customers. Come to the café and have a drink. Wait a little while. She'll be free soon. I promise you, Aisha won't go out with anybody else, until you see her."

Absalem said, "I want to see her now! Now!"

"No! We can't do that. The man she's with already paid."

Absalem Sultane was a quiet man. He was big and strong. But the madman's brother was even larger, and he had a shorter temper too. When he got angry, Absalem decided to leave the house and take a walk.

The big man returned to the café and talked to his brother. "What's wrong with Absalem?" he asked. "Why does he act this way?"

The madman said, "Absalem is in love with the girl Aisha. I suggest that, when he comes to see her, we free her of her other obligations. Absalem Sultane spends a lot of money here. That's what we want."

His brother said, "Yes, it's what we want."

The madman said, "Go back to the house. Tell the patrona that Absalem will return in thirty minutes. Be sure by then that his girlfriend is free."

The big man went back to the whorehouse and told the patrona what his brother said.

Absalem Sultane was a campesino born in the Charf Mountains. He was a quiet man who never said very much. I had seen him before in the whorehouse, sitting in a chair beside the door, waiting until his girlfriend was free. Of course, no man can depend on a whore who's working; she's obligated to any man coming through the door. But Absalem didn't understand this. He loved the girl and refused to accept her profession. He thought of her as the girl of his life, the woman of his dreams, and he spent a lot of money to keep her happy. She was lovely, with long black hair and large brown eyes. Absalem came to see her every

Friday, as soon as he had been paid at work. Now, he was out walking the streets and waiting. After half an hour he returned, and Aisha met him in the hall. He hugged her and kissed her and asked her what she wanted to eat and drink.

She said, "Whatever you want, Absalem. But the next time I'm working when you come, don't make problems. The more problems you make, the more upset the madman and his brother get with me. You know I work here, don't you? You know how big they are."

Absalem Sultane said, "I don't care. I'm not afraid of them. You're my girl. I want to marry you."

Aisha laughed. "You know I can't get married. I'm a whore."

"I don't care," said Absalem. "Will you marry me?"

She said, "Perhaps. If the madman and his brother will let me."

"I'll talk with them," he said. "I'll ask them."

Aisha said, "Not now. We'll do that later, after we go upstairs and talk."

Absalem took Aisha by the hand and they went upstairs to her room on the second floor. A few minutes later, the patrona called in an order to the café, for sodas, roasted chicken and a loaf of bread. The big man filled the order and put it on a tray. I took the tray across the street and went up to the room. Absalem paid me, and tipped me two pesetas. I took the money back to the café and gave it to the madman.

"Was everything all right up there?" he asked.

"Yes," I said. "Everything's all right."

That night Absalem spent two hours with Aisha and paid her a thousand francs an hour. As he was going out he asked again if she would marry him. Aisha said, "If they let me go, I'll marry you tomorrow."

Absalem thought this over. it was Tuesday. "I'll talk to the madman on Friday," he said, "when I get off work. I'll come over here and see what he has to say." Then Absalem left the whorehouse and went home to the mountains. We didn't see him again for three days.

Friday evening Absalem came back to talk to the madman and his brother. He said, "I'm in love with Aisha. I want to marry her."

"No," said the madman. "She's just a whore. What else is she good for?"

Absalem Sultane said he didn't care, he loved her. He wanted to marry her.

The madman's brother said no, too. "She's our best girl. She makes us lots of money. If you marry her, if you take her away, we won't be making money anymore."

Absalem asked them both, "How much? How much money is she worth?"

The madman said, "A half a million francs."

Absalem said he could come up with one hundred thousand. That was all the money he could raise. "What do you say?"

The madman said, "We'll think it over. Come back later."

Absalem left and went across the street to see Aisha. He walked inside, went up to her room, and told her he was going to marry her. He told her how much he had offered the brothers to let her go.

She said, "You're paying all that just for me?"

He said, "You're worth much more than that to me. They asked for half a million. If I had it, I'd give it to them, too. All I can raise is a hundred thousand francs. That's as much as I can pay for you."

She held him close and kissed him and they spent an hour together. When the hour was over, Absalem had to leave. He didn't pay Aisha anything that evening. Aisha paid the thousand francs for him, because he wanted to marry her so badly.

Absalem left the whorehouse and went back to the Charf. He lived in the mountains with one sister, and a father who was very well-to-do. Absalem had nothing more in mind than to marry Aisha.

That night the madman went to see Aisha. "Why did you pay for Absalem's time?" he asked. "Don't forget, you work for *us*." And he hit her, so that her nose bled and her eyes began to swell.

A few days later Absalem came back and saw her face. He said, "What happened?"

"Oh, I fell down," Aisha said. She didn't want to get him into trouble.

Absalem left and went to the café. He asked the madman what had happened.

"Aisha works for us," the madman told him. "She's supposed to turn in everything she earns. Then we give her a percentage."

Absalem understood then what had happened. "You'd better not hit the girl," he said. "The next time I find out she's been beaten, you're going to have to answer to me."

This made the madman so angry that he hit Absalem in the stomach and the face. He kicked him, then he knocked him to the ground. When he was down, he kicked him in the ribs. Finally, the police arrived and stopped it. They took Absalem to a clinic and patched him up.

No one saw him for a week after that.

Late the following Friday he came back, ran into the café with a knife, and attacked the madman, stabbing him everywhere until the madman was bleeding all over his body. The madman's brother was so frightened that he ran to the whorehouse across the street, before he telephoned for the police.

An ambulance arrived and took the madman to the hospital.

It took three days for the wounds to start to heal, but the man's anger wouldn't go away. He made up his mind to leave then, and go looking for Absalem, and no one there was big enough to stop him. He walked all the way from the hospital to the whorehouse, ripping off his bandages as he went. Every wound was bleeding by the time he reached the door. When he fell down in the hallway, the patrona phoned for the police. But before they came, the man had bled to death.

They looked for Absalem everywhere in town, from the Socco Chico to the Socco Kebir. They asked Aisha what she knew about him.

She said, "Nothing. He works in the port. He lives in the Charf Mountains."

"Where in the port does he work?"

She didn't know.

The next morning the police picked up Absalem in the harbor. They took him to the commissariat. Although they held him on a murder charge, the police respected Absalem Sultane. He killed a man they all had been afraid of. He stayed at the commissariat for three days, while the officers completed their report. He confessed he had stabbed the madman many times; but the attack had not killed him, and they knew it. Had the man stayed in his bed, he would be alive now. It was anger that had killed him. When the officers finished their report, they transferred Absalem to the Casbah jail. He stayed there for two months in the prison. Finally, he was called before the court.

The judges charged Absalem with the murder of the madman. Absalem said, "I didn't kill him. I stabbed him as many times as I could manage, but he didn't die."

"Why did you stab him?"

"I was in love with a girl who worked for him. I wanted to marry her. The man asked half a million francs to set her free, and I didn't have it. I offered what I had and went away. A few days later, when I came back, I saw that he had beaten the girl badly. The girl lied about what had happened, to keep me from getting hurt, but I wasn't fooled. When I went to talk with the man, he beat me and kicked me. A week later, I came back with a knife. Then the ambulance took him to the hospital."

"When you came back with your knife, did you mean to kill him?" one judge asked.

Absalem said, "Yes."

"All right. Sit down."

Absalem sat down and the five judges began to talk together.

"Absalem Sultane?"

"Yes?"

"Stand up," they said.

Absalem stood up before the judges and they sentenced him to fifteen years' hard labor. Then they sent him back to the Casbah jail.

Absalem Sultane was very happy. He had killed a man he hated and only received a sentence of fifteen years.

I walked back from the courthouse to the café and found two policemen talking with the owner. Now that the man they feared the most was dead, they knew they could deal with his brother. They made him agree to close down his café and all three whorehouses.

He told me all about it in the morning. ,

"I have no café now," he said, "and no use for you. You'll have to leave and find another job." The women in the houses moved out too.

With the money I'd saved from working there, I went away. I found a vacant storeroom near the mosque, and rented it for two thousand francs a month. This was equal to about four dollars. With some of my money, I bought black market cigarettes and started selling them out on the street.

Chapter Seven

The Careless Man

I bought a carton of cigarettes for four thousand francs, and sold it for six thousand on the street. It took about four hours to sell the carton. On a good day I was able to sell three cartons. This meant a profit of six thousand francs. I thought, This is very good money. I began to save. I was doing well.

Sometimes in the evening I went to Ayeshi's café for tea. The place was a popular hangout for local pimps and thieves. Ayeshi was a strange man. He had lost one eye in a fight and wore a patch. He was very tough, and good at business too. He would buy anything a thief brought in for sale, and he loaned them money, whenever times were hard. When a thief who owed him money stole some goods, Ayeshi was the first in town to know. He got a lot of goods for nothing this way, by calling in his loans, and he made good money running the café. Ayeshi was fairly well-to-do. He owned three houses in the city, two ranches, and an orchard outside town near Malabata. I went to his place from time to time to sit with the other men there, play cards and dominoes, tell jokes and listen.

One evening a man named Moreno brought four balls of cheese to the café. The balls were sealed with red wax all around them. He showed them to Ayeshi and said they were for sale. I watched him set the large balls on the counter.

Ayeshi looked at them. He said, "It's too much cheese. It

would spoil, before I had a chance to sell it."

Moreno said, "No. If you don't cut them up, they will last a long, long time."

"What do you want for them?" Ayeshi asked.

"Ten thousand francs."

"That's too much."

"All right, give me eight thousand," Moreno said.

"No. I'll give you six."

"Ouakha," said Moreno. "Give me the money."

Moreno took the money and went out. He had a good meal down the street, then came back again to play some cards. Ayeshi went on serving tea and dealing with the thieves who came to see him. He set the balls of cheese behind the counter.

I left around midnight, went to my room and fell asleep. Three nights later, I returned to the café and found Moreno working for Ayeshi.

I said, "What happened? Where's Ayeshi?"

"Ayeshi? He went out to his orchard for a few days. He left me here, in charge. What can I do for you?"

I ordered a glass of tea and joined some men at one of the tables, playing dominoes. I played until about one o'clock that night. Then I went back to my room, made tea on the little stove there, and fell asleep. In the morning, I went to my distributor to buy more cigarettes. He wasn't legally licensed to do this work, but he had three boats, and every evening they sailed to Tangier from Gibraltar loaded down with English cigarettes. It was late before I reached his place that day. He didn't have much merchandise on hand. I bought one carton, paid him, and went back to my room. There I opened the carton, put four packs of cigarettes in my pockets, and walked down to the Socco Chico.

I sold the first two packs and had two left, when two policemen came around the corner. I'd been set up, but I didn't know it yet. They put their handcuffs on me in the square.

"You're selling black market cigarettes," they said.

"I'm not."

"You're lying."

I said, "I'm not. That's the truth."

They locked me up for three hours in a cell, then took me upstairs to an inspector. "What do you have to say for yourself?" he asked. "Are you selling cigarettes illegally?"

"No sir, I'm not. I bought these cigarettes to smoke myself."

He slapped me. "Tell the truth."

"I told you. That's the truth."

"We'll keep the cigarettes," he said. "You're going to pay a fine—ten thousand francs."

"Why am I paying for cigarettes I bought to smoke myself?"

"They're English cigarettes," he said. "They have no government seal. Can't you see?"

"I don't know anything about that. I've told you all I know."

"Are you going to pay ten thousand francs, or do you want to serve ten days in prison?"

I agreed to pay the fine. They let me go.

I left the commissariat and went back to the Socco Chico. By the time I had returned, the word was out. The regular sellers had tried to have me busted. They'd decided I wasn't fit to do business in their territory.

One asked me what the officers had done.

I said, "They took my cigarettes. They made me pay a fine and they let me go."

"You shouldn't be hanging around here selling cigarettes," he said. "We've been selling a long time in the Socco. We don't want any strangers butting in."

I said, "Don't worry. I won't come here again. But you're not going to stop me from making a living. Did I tell the police about you guys?"

He said, "Of course not."

"Then why did you tell the police about me?"

He said, "I told you. We don't want strangers coming in."

I promised them I wouldn't come back again. "Tangier is big," I said. "There's room for everyone."

I walked to my room and picked up the remaining six packs of cigarettes. I put them in my pocket and went to the Spanish church across the street. When people passed, I asked them if they wanted discount cigarettes. I took about an hour to sell six packs. By then I had some money in my pocket. When it started raining, I decided not to bother with more cigarettes that day. I went to my room, made tea, and ate some cheese and bread. I listened to radio music for a while and fell asleep there.

In the morning I went down to the harbor where the Spanish ferries docked and helped people carry off their suitcases. I decided not to buy or sell any cigarettes for a while. I made five or six hundred francs a day in the harbor. It was enough.

A few days later I stopped in at Ayeshi's. I ordered tea and started playing cards. An hour later six police came in. They said, "Everybody stay where you are!" They searched the place, until they found Moreno.

"Your name's Moreno?"

"Yes."

"Come with us."

They put cuffs on him and began to lead him off.

"If I go," he said, "there's no one here to manage the café. Ayeshi left me in charge."

"Don't worry about Ayeshi," they told him. "Ayeshi's in jail himself."

The officers made everybody leave. They locked the door, handed the key to Moreno and took him away with them.

The café had been closed at least three days, before I heard the story of the cheese. Ayeshi had taken one of the four balls home with him, and cut it open. Under the wax he found, not cheese, but money. Moreno's balls of cheese were full of francs, in bills worth ten thousand francs apiece. In all, the four cheese balls contained two million francs. Ayeshi had gone out the following morning to his favorite café on the mountain. Ayeshi only went there when he wanted to indulge himself completely. The café belonged to two French sisters. Everything was very expensive there. Ayeshi was drunk when he arrived. He tossed his cash around without a care, lit cigarettes with the big bills, and drew a lot of attention to himself. The sisters saw immediately that something wasn't right. They had seen Ayeshi here before, but he'd never lit his cigarettes with money. They phoned the authorities. The police arrived and took him to the commissariat.

They asked Ayeshi where he got his money.

"It's mine. I worked for it," he said.

"If you worked for it, why were you burning it all up?"

They handcuffed him. They drove him to his orchard near Malabata. They searched his house and found the two million francs, boxed it up, and brought him back to jail. Two hundred thousand francs were missing. This was bcause Ayeshi had paid ten thousand francs apiece for the sisters' drinks. Each drink cost five hundred. The other nine thousand five hundred was his tip.

Ayeshi and Moreno stayed in the Casbah jail for ten days. Then they were called to the tribunal.

The judges questioned Moreno first: "Where did you get this money?"

"I stole cheese, not money," Moreno said.

The judges asked him what he'd sold the cheese for.

"Six thousand francs," Moreno said.

"You sold two million francs for six thousand?"

"I didn't know what it was," Moreno said. "If I'd known that it was money, why would I sell it?"

"Sit down," they said.

Next they asked Ayeshi, "What happened to the missing two hundred thousand francs?"

"Some I spent," he said, "and some I burned."

They asked Moreno where he had found the cheese.

He said, "I broke into the trunk of a French sedan. The cheese was in the trunk. I thought I'd find some luggage, or some clothes. There were only the balls of cheese. So, I stole the cheese."

The judges said, "Both of you sit down."

The five judges discussed the case together, then they had the men stand up again. They gave Moreno six months in prison. They gave Ayeshi nine months, for buying stolen goods.

When both men had been sentenced, the judges said, "Moreno, what is the most money you've ever had at one time in your hands?"

"Ten thousand francs," Moreno said.

They fined Moreno this amount, in addition to his sentence. Then the police took both of them away.

Ayeshi's café stayed closed while he served his sentence. When nine months had passed and he got out, he went back into business as before. But he had changed. Now, he was more serious.

I saw him a few days after he got out. I went up to his counter and I said, "Hello, Ayeshi. How does it feel to have two million francs and not know what to do with them?"

He said, "Don't talk to me about that stupid money! I've suffered for it. Just tell me what you want."

I ordered a glass of tea, and sat down and kept away from him. I could see he was in no mood to talk about it. He was just another careless man who'd had a fortune and no idea what to do about it.

Today and tomorrow, time went by. I went on hustling smuggled cigarettes, because I made more that way than by working in the harbor. I thought it was easy. I kept at it.

Chapter Eight

The Child Killer

One afternoon I went up to the Socco Kebir, where all the local buses come and go. An old man was mixing with the crowds there, asking for information about his son. The boy was a five-year-old. He'd been gone two days. The father suspected he'd been kidnapped. The police had searched for him and had no luck. Finally, the old man put up a reward of two hundred thousand francs, for anyone who led him to his son. Now, the man was out walking among the people. "Ladies and gentlemen," the father cried, and he showed two photos of his son and told the story.

The father of the boy was called Jamil. He'd been born in the Rif in the city of Melilla and had come to town when he was fourteen. After Morocco gained its independence, Jamil took over a Spanish café across from the bus station and started into business. By now, he was known all over town, a successful man who owned three sewing shops and five cafés, as well as two or three houses around the city. Jamil employed a lot of local people. The missing boy was the only son he had.

The people of Tangier began to think about his reward. Two hundred thousand francs was a lot. Jamil announced the sum around the station, then he walked downhill to the Socco Chico and announced it there. Three days passed, and things were still the same. No one could tell him a thing about the boy.

Five days later some children, playing in the European quarter, saw a line of ants climb the side of a building to a closed window on the second floor. The children shouted and pointed and began to kill the ants, as a sort of game, until the landlord came and chased them off. A few minutes later they came back and began again. This time the landlord saw the window and went upstairs to check the door. The apartment belonged to a man named Nazir. He had come to town from Fez after Independence, and rose through the administrative ranks, until he became the Minister of Transportation. Nazir was much respected in Tangier. That morning when the landlord opened up the flat, he found the body of a child lying dead there. The sight was horrible. The body had been locked up for a week.

The landlord ran downstairs and called the police. They arrived with an ambulance and had the boy taken to the hospital. But there was nothing anyone could do.

The police went from the hospital to Jamil's café. When they came in, Jamil said, "Where is my son? Have you found him?"

They said, "Sidi Jamil, we think your son is dead. Will you come with us to the hospital? Someone must identify the body. The way things are, we can't be sure."

Jamil went to the hospital with the officers. He looked at the corpse and said it was his son. The boy had a piece of candy in his hand. There was blood on his buttocks. Sidi Jamil fainted when he saw this. He knew now what had happened to his son. There are plenty of men in the world who lie to boys, and buy them bits of candy. A man can give a child something sweet, and take his life, and the child will never even notice.

The police revived Jamil. At first he was too angry to stand up. "What kind of man could do this to my son?"

The police returned Jamil to his café. Then they went to the Bureau of Transportation and picked up the minister from Fez. They took him to the commissariat and locked him in a cell.

Jamil had lost the only son he had. He told everyone that came
to the café how the boy had died, and the people became as angry
as Jamil. That afternoon, they organized a march on the commissariat. They planned to seize the minister themselves, pour
gas on him and burn the man alive.

By four o'clock a thousand men were marching through the
streets toward the commissariat. The building stood at the top of
twenty stairs in the Socco Kebir, next to the hospital emergency
room. People came from all over the city, when they heard what
had happened to Jamil. They couldn't stand it. I saw men with
cans of gasoline; others carried bottles in their hands. They were
ready to punish this man for what he'd done. Soon they had the
commissariat surrounded. There were only a handful of officers
on guard, but the word went out, and soon enough policemen
posted all around the city rushed back to headquarters. Those
who were off duty came from their homes. Before long, there
were hundreds of policemen and thousands of people in the
square.

The crowd on the stairs surged forward to break in and seize
the minister. The police did what they could to drive them back.
The Governor of Tangier arrived, saw the size of the crowd, and
called the army. Twenty minutes later there were soldiers everywhere around the prison. They unshouldered their rifles in the
crowd. Then the Governor made an announcement through a
bullhorn: *Go home! You must go home now! You must leave
justice to the law!*

The crowd cried back: *What law is this? Did it protect our
children? Who is this man you're holding in your cell? We don't
want a man like that living in Tangier!*

The Governor refused to give the prisoner's name. The people
refused to go away. Then he gave a signal to the army, and the
soldiers fired tear gas on the crowd. The people scattered running

in every direction and the soldiers followed, chasing them away. Soon there was nothing left on the square, but overturned cans and broken bottles of gasoline running out like water on the street. One man with a matchstick could have turned the whole town to a burning hell.

The soldiers remained all evening in the Socco. They were still there in the morning, and so were the police. The police were everywhere. You couldn't go ten steps without passing an officer.

I walked past the commissariat to Jamil's café, but it was closed. People arrived and tapped at the door all day, to bring their condolences, but Jamil was in his home and refused to see them. His family was in a state of shock. Meanwhile, the people were holding meetings. They met in large numbers inside the mosques, to avoid suspicion, and tried to agree on what to do. They thought it would be best to wait a while, to watch the commissariat. When things cooled off, they planned to storm the jail, kill anyone who tried to keep them out, seize the man who had killed the boy, and burn him to death there in the Socco. They wanted everyone to see him burning.

The Governor's spies were everywhere, of course. It wasn't possible to say a word, without the authorities knowing all about it. When the Governor found out about the plot, he and his men decided to transfer the prisoner to Rabat, and try him there in the capital hundreds of miles from Tangier. At three o'clock that morning a wagon came, the minister stepped in, they drove away.

The next day the crowds returned to the commissariat. They demanded to see the prisoner again. They wanted the right to question him, they said, to find out why he'd attacked a child and murdered him.

The police chief said, "The prisoner isn't here."

"Where did he go?"

"We can't tell you that. He's been transferred somewhere, for his trial. Don't worry! I swear to Allah, the man will get what's coming to him. Go back home now, all of you! Leave justice to the law. He'll get his due."

The crowd screamed back, *This isn't justice! Why not try him here, where the crime was done! We have plenty of courtrooms in Tangier. Why was he transferred?*

The chief said, "It wasn't my idea. It came from higher up. I work for someone too, the way we all do. Please! Go home! Don't make things more horrible than they are. It's a shame that this has happened. But the matter is no longer in my hands."

The crowd formed into long lines and marched on the Governor's office. There were several thousand people in the streets now. The policemen went ahead, diverting cars, sending the traffic away from the path of the marchers. The people walked until they reached the office of the Governor. They circled the building for several hours. Finally, the Governor came to his window. He used a microphone to address the crowds, pleading with the people to go home. *This isn't right!* he cried. *You're trying to take the law into your hands. Some of you will be hurt, if this keeps up. If you don't leave now, I'll call the soldiers. They'll do what they did last night, if you don't go home.*

The people talked it over among themselves and agreed to leave. They moved in great streams through the open streets, until the grounds around the office were deserted. Only soldiers and bureaucrats were left.

I walked back to the Socco after that. There were dozens of buses loading on the square, taking people back to their homes in every part of the city. I watched them leave, then walked downhill into the Socco Chico. I went up to my room there and made a glass of tea. I didn't go out again that afternoon.

In the morning I got up early and walked through town. I didn't sell any cigarettes that day. I was tired, and sick of the police who chased me whenever they saw me. They hadn't found any cigarettes on me lately. I'd been lucky. I walked up to the Socco Kebir instead. I passed the bus station. Sidi Jamil's café there was still closed, but hundreds of people had come by, bringing gifts. When a child dies in Morocco, friends often bring the family food—dates, figs, butter, buttermilk, bread, and money, to help the family cope with what has happened. Today, the people found the door still locked. They left their gifts on the steps of the café. I saw great piles of food there, and a basket overflowing with coins and bills.

Three days later, a funeral was held. Thousands of people came from all over the city, to take turns bearing the coffin through the streets. Every few minutes, four new men stepped up and took the handles of the coffin. Sympathy and sorrow for Jamil flowed into every corner of Tangier. Jamil walked at the head of the wooden bier, crying all the way to the cemetery. There the boy was buried on a hill. A holy man said a prayer for him. When it was done, food appeared for the poor people in the crowds. The food, spread out on blankets, covered a large part of the grounds. This was something Moslems always do. When someone dies, they give food to the poor—figs, dates, fruit, and milk and bread. If they have any money on them, they give that too. The people ate and ate, and when they stopped, there were still many trays of food unfinished.

When the feasting stopped, Sidi Jamil stood up on the grave and thanked the whole city for its kindness. Then he walked down into the streets again toward his home. Soon, the cemetery was deserted.

A week went by. Then Jamil opened all his businesses again. He went on his way, as he always had. Time passed slowly, today and tomorrow, month by month by month.

One day two or three years later, an article appeared in the local newspaper. The Minister of Transportation finally had been sentenced to thirty years' hard labor for his crime. The night he went into prison in Rabat, the inmates in the jail discussed his case. On Friday, the Moslem holy day, they said the prayer for the dead and went to sleep. The guards found the minister in the morning. He was still in bed. His throat had been cut from ear to ear. An article appeared in the Tangier news, saying that the man who had killed the boy was dead himself, killed by all the prisoners in his cell.

The people of Tangier didn't believe it. They could not be sure—they saw no photos of the dead man with his throat cut. They went to the Governor's office in a crowd, demanding he send a delegation, to verify what had happened in Rabat. The Governor agreed to send ten men to view the body. Two days later, a bus arrived in the Socco and took the delegation to Rabat. When the men returned, they went to see Jamil.

"We've been to the morgue and seen the man," they told him. "Allah has taken his life from him for murdering your son. He has given you justice."

Jamil thanked the men and they said good-bye and everyone went on his way again.

OTHER TITLES FROM TOMBOUCTOU

Late Returns, Tom Clark, 96 pages, 7.00
The Timing Chain, Douglas Woolf, 136 pages, 7.00
Phantom Pain, Lucia Berlin, 120 pages, 7.00
Convivio: New College Journal of Poetics, #1, John Thorpe, editor, 120 pages, 7.00
The Chest, Mohammed Mrabet, 100 pages, 7.50
Sunday, Phoebe MacAdams, 100 pages, 6.00
Neighbors, Stephen Emerson, 94 pages, 6.00
Beautiful Phantoms, Barry Gifford, 80 pages, 5.00
The Japan & India Journals, Joanne Kyger, 300 pages, 10.00
American Ones, Clark Coolidge, 48 pages, 5.00
Practicing, Jamie MacInnis, 64 pages, 5.00
Five Aces & Independence, John Thorpe, 120 pages, 5.00
No, You Wore Red, Michael Wolfe, 64 pages, 5.00
Wild Cherries, Dale Herd, 88 pages, 5.00
Shit On My Shoes, Duncan McNaughton, 120 pages, 5.00
This Eating & Walking, Leslie Scalapino, 56 pages, 3.00
The Air's Nearly Perfect Elasticity, Richard Duerden, 118 pages, 3.50
Shameless, Jim Gustafson, 64 pages, 3.00
The Basketball Diaries, Jim Carroll, 156 pages, 4.00
How I Broke In, Tom Clark, 80 pages, 3.00
Stories & Poems, Gailyn Saroyan, 48 pages, 2.25
Frenchy & Cuban Pete, Bobbie Louise Hawkins, 80 pages, 3.00
Sumeriana, Duncan McNaughton, 80 pages, 3.00
FIVE, Lawrence Kearney, 80 pages, 3.00
News from Niman Farm, Lewis MacAdams, 48 pages, 2.50

DESERT ISLAND CHAPBOOK SERIES

New York Notes, Stephen Ratcliffe, 24 pages, 3.00
Start Over, Bill Berkson, 32 pages, 3.50
Let Us Not Blame Foolish Women, Dotty leMieux, 24 pages, 3.50
Triggers, Donald Guravich, 32 pages, 3.50

Lise Knox-Seith
(415) 494-8306

Zeta Magazine
116 St. Botolph St
Boston, MA 02115-9479